SPIDER-MAN®
CARNAGE IN NEW YORK

SPIDER-MAN: THE VENOM FACTOR
by Diane Duane

THE ULTIMATE SPIDER-MAN
Stan Lee, Editor

IRON MAN: THE ARMOR TRAP
by Greg Cox

SPIDER-MAN: CARNAGE IN NEW YORK
by David Michelinie & Dean Wesley Smith

THE INCREDIBLE HULK: WHAT SAVAGE BEAST
by Peter David

SPIDER-MAN: THE LIZARD SANCTION
by Diane Duane

THE ULTIMATE SILVER SURFER
Stan Lee, Editor

FANTASTIC FOUR: TO FREE ATLANTIS
by Nancy A. Collins

DAREDEVIL: PREDATOR'S SMILE
by Christopher Golden

X-MEN: MUTANT EMPIRE: Book 1: SIEGE
by Christopher Golden

THE ULTIMATE SUPER-VILLAINS
Stan Lee, Editor

SPIDER-MAN & THE INCREDIBLE HULK: RAMPAGE
by Danny Fingeroth & Eric Fein (Doom's Day Book 1)

SPIDER-MAN: GOBLIN'S REVENGE
by Dean Wesley Smith

THE ULTIMATE X-MEN
Stan Lee, Editor

Coming soon:

SPIDER-MAN: THE OCTOPUS AGENDA
by Diane Duane

X-MEN: MUTANT EMPIRE: Book 2: SANCTUARY
by Christopher Golden

IRON MAN: OPERATION A.I.M.
by Greg Cox

David Michelinie &
Dean Wesley Smith

Illustrations by James W. Fry & Keith Aiken

BYRON PREISS MULTIMEDIA COMPANY, INC.
NEW YORK

BOULEVARD BOOKS, NEW YORK

Special thanks to Lou Aronica, Eric Fein, Danny Fingeroth, and Julia Molino.

SPIDER-MAN: CARNAGE IN NEW YORK

A Boulevard Book
A Byron Preiss Multimedia Company, Inc. Book

PRINTING HISTORY
Boulevard edition / August 1995

Edited by Keith R.A. DeCandido.
Cover art by Julie Bell.
Cover design by Claude Goodwin.
Interior design by Todd Sutherland.

For information address: Byron Preiss Multimedia Company, Inc., 24 West 25th Street, New York, New York 10010.

ISBN: 1-57297-019-7

BOULEVARD
Boulevard Books are published by The Berkley Publishing Group, 200 Madison Avenue, New York, New York 10016.

PRINTED IN THE UNITED STATES OF AMERICA

10 9 8 7 6 5 4

For Mouse
—DM

For Janie and Lenny.
And for Nina, who bought
a lot of comics from me
over the years.
—DWS

CHAPTER I

CARNAGE IN NEW YORK

The cold October air bites hard at midnight.

The streets of the city are slick and black with rain and have lost what little heat they gathered during the day. The dark shoves the city lights into small circular islands of false safety on the sidewalks, like spotlights on a Broadway stage.

At midnight in October, the fall's misty rain cuts through unprotected hands and nips at cheeks and faces with an intensity forgotten in the hot days of summer. Breath is frosty-white in the air and the chill makes teeth chatter.

Winter is on the way and it sneaks up on the city at night, one cold, biting step at a time.

Dr. Eric Catrall paid little attention to the cold and the light rain cutting through his tan overcoat and his bare white hands. Instead he glanced left, then quickly right at the deserted sidewalks of 92nd Street as he ducked around the corner of a deli and moved away from the brighter lights of Broadway. Through the mist on his glasses he was watching for much, much worse than anything the weather could do to him.

He clutched his black briefcase to his chest with his icy hands as the sounds of his dress shoes clicking on the wet pavement echoed up through the tall buildings and off the closed, dark windows. He feared losing the briefcase almost more than losing his own life. One minute he wanted to just toss the black leather monster into the nearest dumpster and run to forget it ever existed. Then the next minute the simple thought of losing the case and its contents would send his heart racing out of control and his breathing into panicked gulps for air.

The briefcase and its contents were tearing him apart and somewhere deep down inside he knew he couldn't last much longer.

But at the same time, he knew he didn't have a choice.

A cold gust of wind snapped at his coat and hair and he thought he heard other footsteps. He glanced quickly over his shoulder and then around at the dark street. No one was in sight.

He suddenly stopped and listened, hoping to catch his pursuers moving. Hoping to hear their steps or the sounds of their breathing in the cold night air.

Nothing.

Nothing but the silence of the dark, wet street, the distant honking of cabs on Broadway and the heavy pounding of his own heart.

He was as alone as a person could be in Manhattan.

When he started again the loud sounds of his

own steps panicked him and he started to run, then slowed to a fast walk after a few paces, his breath coming in large, hard gasps. He wanted to tip-toe, move like a ghost through the streets, but he didn't have the time. He had to keep going.

Walk fast, maybe even run.

He had to get away.

He had to get to a safe place and figure out what to do. His life, and a lot of other lives, depended on what he did next.

A raised edge of sidewalk caught the toe of his shoe and he stumbled forward. His left hand shot out and he came very close to smashing the briefcase against a staircase railing that led down into a basement apartment.

At the last instant he managed to catch himself, yanking the briefcase sideways, only grazing it against the metal.

Close. Way too close. He needed to be more careful.

He clutched the case to his chest, afraid he would hear the contents. If he could hear the contents, then it was broken and all was lost.

If he could hear the contents then thousands would die, all because of him.

But nothing rattled in the case and he let out a deep sigh and again glanced around. He needed to get off this street, cut down an alley, find a subway, get out of the city. Anything.

He studied the black doorways.

He studied the stairs along the sidewalks going down into more blackness.

He studied the sidewalk and street stretching in front of him.

Then he saw it. Straight ahead loomed a black slot between two stately old apartment buildings. An alley. That would work. He would cut down it to 93rd, and hide across the street to see if anyone followed him. If they did, they would have to come out of the alley and he would see them.

If no one followed him through the alley he would circle around and go back to the little hotel he had passed off 90th Street. Then, after a night's sleep, he might be able to figure out what to do.

He started walking again, slowly, controlled. Taking shallow breaths, he listened for any other movement on the street. He had a plan now and the sanity of the plan helped clear his mind.

At the face of the alley he kept going, pretending he was going to pass the corridor. Then at the last instant he ducked to the right and down the deserted alleyway.

He stopped in the first shadow and listened, his heart pounding in his ears, his breath sending white clouds of mist into the air around him. No one seemed to be following him. But he didn't want to let himself believe that. He couldn't be that lucky. Not after what he had done. He'd get to the next street and hide and watch just to make sure.

He turned and moved quickly down the alley, using only the glow from a few windows and the distant streetlights to guide him through the garbage cans and dumpsters. The place smelled of rotten cabbage and a dead animal. The rain brought out the smells on the pavement, accentuated them. They choked him slightly.

After a hundred steps, he looked up into the looming face of a dark brick wall. The alley was a dead end. A building sat there, almost tauntingly, its blank brick wall disappearing into the black night. He clutched the briefcase to his chest and breathed quickly, glancing up, down, sideways, hoping against hope for a way out of the alley. He couldn't have let himself get trapped like this. It wasn't possible. There had to be a way out.

Any way at all.

But there was nothing but a few locked doors, brick walls, and garbage.

"Oh, no," he said softly to himself, his heart feeling like it might explode at any moment. He was trapped again. He had to get back to the street.

He was halfway to the opening of the alley when two men stepped into the light from the street and closed off his escape. He could see that they were wearing business suits, open rain coats, and fedoras.

But he couldn't see their faces and that dug at his mind like nothing else could.

Their presence filled the alley like the worst nightmare from his childhood. The nightmare of his dead father standing in his bedroom door, the hall light behind him, his face totally dark.

Now two men blocked his path and he couldn't see their faces no matter how hard he looked.

Inside him something snapped and he panicked, his mind screaming that he had to escape at all costs.

His gaze darted at every door, every opening of the alley, but there was no escape except right through the two men.

They stood watching him.

Silent.

Ominous.

If there was no escape, then he would face his fear.

He would face his dead father and the nightmares that filled his life after the man died.

He would face them all right now.

He spotted a short length of lead pipe and quickly picked it up, hardly noticing the cold wet feel of it in his hand. The pipe gave him strength. He could feel the extra courage coursing up his arm and though his system.

He had never won with the nightmares of his dead father standing in his bedroom door. His doctors, his mother, no one could stop the vision that had haunted him. The visions had beat him as a kid. But this time he would win.

With the briefcase clutched as tightly as he could hold it in his left hand and the pipe in the other, he started forward, his stride firm, his gaze focused on the space between them and the light and seeming safety of the street beyond.

The man on the doctor's right extended a hand like a ghost pointing at a grave. A low, powerful voice echoed down the closed alley. "Give us the briefcase, Dr. Catrall. Give us the briefcase and no one gets hurt."

The doctor paid no attention.

He just kept moving at them.

It was one of those cold nights in the city that made Spider-Man wonder why anyone would want to be out. And more than that, he wondered what in the world he was doing out.

The hard rain from earlier in the evening had cut back to a fine, cold mist that made every building, every street, every car seem extra cold. The entire city felt dark and forbidding.

He'd enjoyed the summer, hot and humid as it had been. At least in the summer his fingers didn't freeze and his feet weren't always cold like they were in the winter. He wasn't looking forward to the coming snow at all. Being a super hero in a snowstorm was not a great deal of fun and for the last few years he had wondered why he didn't just take the winter off. But so far he hadn't. And now fall was here. Fall was the first cold and the first sign winter was coming. Fall for Spidey was just an all-around depressing time.

Midnight. He crouched on a high stone ledge under a wide roof overhang, doing his best to stay dry, his camera safely covered on the ledge beside him.

Earlier in the evening he'd been trailing a reported mob boss, trying to get pictures of the jerk for the *Daily Bugle.* He and his wife Mary Jane needed the extra money those pictures would bring. He had decided it had been easier and safer to do the trailing as Spider-Man and he'd followed the guy for two hours, getting a few pictures, but nothing special enough.

At least not the kind of pictures J. Jonah Jameson wanted to publish. He wanted the pictures of the mob boss with a politician's wife, or the guy taking money, or shooting someone. So far the best picture Spidey had managed to get was the guy sitting in Carmine's shoving a large forkful of meatballs into his wide mouth. Real front-page material there.

And the evening had not gotten better. Two

hours ago, the mobster had gone into a building on Broadway, across the street from where Spider-Man now sat. Two long hours of sitting on a cold ledge in the rain. Midnight and it seemed like the photo-shoot was over. The guy wasn't coming out, and the pictures weren't worth Spidey going in.

From his perch on the ledge, Spider-Man overlooked the traffic on Broadway and could see down four other side streets. Through his boots, he could feel his feet going numb from the cold. Mary Jane would be at home in bed, cuddled under the blankets, warm and toasty. She'd yell at him when he crawled in and touched her with his cold feet. But at night her body was like a heater and it wouldn't take him long to warm up next to her. That was one of the things he loved about her. One of the many things.

And right now that heater ability of hers sounded real good.

"Human heater, here I come," he said to the cold night air and tucked his camera away safely into his carry pouch. "Hope she's got the furnace turned up high."

He was about to shoot a web at the nearest building and swing for home when something caught his eye, yanking his attention away from the warm thoughts of Mary Jane and to the sidewalks of Broadway below.

A man with a light tan overcoat and a black

briefcase was moving along quickly, his head twisting back and forth as if he thought he was being followed, but couldn't see by whom. He moved like a panicked man, his motions jerky and unsure.

Spidey leaned over and studied the guy. He was stocky, with a bald spot on the top of his head. Spidey guessed him to be in his mid-forties, the office type that should be home in Brooklyn in front of the fire on this kind of night.

As Spidey watched, the guy turned up 92nd and disappeared into the shadows between the streetlights.

Wonder what that was all about? Spider-Man thought. Then he spied two other men in dark coats and fedoras turning up the same street, following the guy.

These two stayed in the shadows along the buildings and moved with the confidence of professionals who had stalked a lot of game through the jungles of the city. They fit in with the dark night very well and looked right at home on the street compared to the guy they were following.

Problems, Spidey thought. *That's what it's about. Lots of problems.*

Spidey hit the nearest building with a web and swung off the ledge silently, heading down the dark street after the three, staying above them and out of sight.

The guy with the briefcase tripped and suddenly stopped.

The two following him stopped exactly at the same time. They were obviously very good at tracking in the city, better than Spidey had first guessed. They were perfectly silent and stayed in the exact places where their prey couldn't see them. Real professionals, of that there was no doubt. But who were they working for?

And why this guy?

Spidey, he admonished himself, *your curiosity is going to get you in trouble here.*

But, of course, Spidey didn't listen to himself. He stayed up on the top ledges of the buildings and made sure he made no sound. The two guys doing the tracking looked good enough to spot him if he moved wrongly.

The panicked guy with the briefcase obviously knew, or could sense, the two men were there behind him. Without warning, he suddenly ducked down an alley.

Nice choice there, Spider-Man thought from his perch at the top of the building. *That's a dead end.*

He swung down the side of the building and then moved silently to a spot above the mouth of the alley. He stayed to the shadows and it was clear none of the men below knew he was watching.

The guy with the briefcase quickly discovered it

was a cul-de-sac. Like a trapped animal he looked for another way out. Spidey just shook his head. He could see the two men approaching the alley.

"Better hurry," he said under his breath, cheering the trapped man on.

The guy started up the alley, but the two men in hats stepped into the entrance, blocking it before he was even halfway there.

Oops. Just not fast enough. Spidey started working his way down the side of the building.

The guy with the briefcase picked up a piece of metal pipe and started at the two like a bull charging blindly at a cape.

Mister, you're nuts, Spidey thought.

"Give us the briefcase, Dr. Catrall," one of the guys said. "Give us the briefcase and no one gets hurt."

"Wow," Spider-Man said in a loud voice. "This neighborhood is sure getting a better class of muggers these days. Those suits look like Armanis."

The guy with the pipe stopped like he'd walked into a stone wall and all three glanced around. Spider-Man dropped off the wall to the ground between them and faced the two guys with hats.

"Don't you two know that you shouldn't bother doctors when they're trying to make a house call?"

The man on the right stepped forward. "This is

none of your business, Spider-Man." His hand reached inside his coat.

Spidey's spider-sense tingled, instantly warning him the guy had a weapon. He might be a good tracker, but he was as dumb as he looked.

Instinctively Spidey flipped straight forward in a tight tumbling flip and caught the guy in the chest with both feet, shoving him backward. The kick left two wet footprints on the guy's clean coat.

Spidey did a quick back-handspring off the cold pavement and came up standing.

"Looks like it's the dry cleaners for that coat tomorrow," Spidey said, brushing the water off his hands as the guy tumbled on the wet concrete and landed in a garbage can. "Don't bother to send me the bill."

The second man ducked behind a dumpster and pulled out a Taser launcher. There was a slight high-pitched ringing sound, then he fired.

Spidey did a quick back-flip up onto the wall, letting the electric darts hit uselessly against the bricks with a few sparks that lit up the alley.

Spider-Man dropped back to the concrete surface just as the first guy recovered enough to pull a stun gun from his pocket. But he didn't get a chance to use it, as Spidey let loose with a barrage of webbing that encased the man from neck to knees. The man tried to keep his balance, but wound up stumbling into a full garbage can, burying him in fish bones, spoiled cabbage and other unspeakable and smelly things.

"Whew!" Spidey said, waving his hand in front of his mask. "Now you really need to clean that coat. And the rest of you could use a bath, too."

He turned to the guy behind the dumpster who still held the Taser. "You want to try that again?"

Sure enough, and a little to Spidey's surprise, the guy lifted the weapon. Again it hummed like an early warning system right before he fired the electric darts. Not a very good weapon for surprise attacks, that was for sure. Especially against someone with his own built-in warning system.

Spidey just ducked, letting the darts hit the bricks in a shower of sparks again.

Then he crossed the alley with two quick leaps. He grabbed a half-empty garbage can and jumped up on the dumpster behind the guy. Before he even had a chance to cover his head or move in any direction, Spidey dropped the can upside down over him.

Then Spider-Man jumped into the middle of the alley and stood over the two men, half laughing as they fought to dig their way out of the smelly and slippery mess. " 'Garbage in, garbage out,' as the old saying goes."

The guy who wasn't all webbed up stood slowly

and brushed off some of the stinking vegetables, then reached into his jacket through the rotten and sticky milk.

Spider-Man moved to stop him, then realized his spider-sense wasn't warning him of danger. The guy wasn't going for another weapon. He was stupid, but not that stupid, it seemed.

Slowly, being careful to move deliberately, the guy pulled out his wallet with two fingers and flipped it open.

Inside, Spidey saw that the guy worked for the government. FBI agent, to be exact. The guy held the wallet out long enough for Spidey to see the badge and identification clearly in the dim light of the alley. As he did so, the other guy got the garbage can off his head and stood.

"Catrall's gone!"

Both agents quickly scanned the alley as Spider-Man watched. He really didn't want to tell them that the good doctor had left as soon as they started firing the fancy guns. It was better that the doctor had a good running start.

The one with the badge turned to Spider-Man. "You've got a lot of explaining to do, Mister."

"Uh, I have only one thing to say to you two." Spidey grasped his nose through his mask. "Get a shower. You both need it. Bye."

He scampered nimbly up the wall and over the top of the building into the darkness.

What a strange night it had been. No good photos, therefore no money. And then mixing it up with the FBI. He'd give it some thought in the morning. But now, cuddling up next to Mary Jane was going to feel great after all this.

It took him only a minute to retrieve his camera from the ledge. Five minutes later his cold feet touched Mary Jane's and she squealed in protest.

It felt great to be home.

The thick smell of rancid grease filled the dark alley two blocks from where the FBI agents stood, trying to get the tiny pieces of rotten cabbage out of their hair.

Dr. Catrall paid little attention to the smell of the alley. His hands were trembling, but not from the cold. That was too close a call. It was lucky the web-slinger was there to help him, but next time he might not be so lucky.

He sat on the wet pavement behind the dumpster and put the briefcase across his knees. With numb fingers he opened both locks with faint clicks and lifted the lid just enough to see inside.

The foam-lined interior of the case was a steel gray that swallowed the faint light. In the center of the case was a single glass vial filled with amber liquid that caught the night light and seemed to intensify it. Dr. Catrall stared at the vial for a moment as if hypnotized, then closed and locked the case again.

He clutched the case to his chest and closed his eyes, letting the smells and the darkness of the alley cover and protect him for the moment.

The vial was still intact.

And because it was, he was still the most dangerous man in the world.

CHAPTER 2

High in the Colorado Rockies, a rock-walled valley had already felt the coming of fall. The trees that dotted the dead-end canyon had all lost their leaves; the only green remaining was that of the pine trees and a light cover of winter grass.

In the middle of this valley was a large, windowless, gray building that sat inside a tall, high voltage fence. No plant or tree was allowed to grow within a hundred yards of the fence or anywhere inside.

Only a few small rocks and concrete sidewalks marred the smoothness of the ground between the building and the fence.

A hundred yards outside the fence sat four guard towers, peppered around the top and down the sides with machine guns and high-powered lasers, all aimed inward at the gray building known as the Vault.

The Vault was a super prison designed and built for the sole reason of holding super-powered criminals. And on this fall day, its most infamous inmate was a skinny man named Cletus Kasady.

The Vault's paranormal inmates necessitated paranormal guards, hence the Guardsmen. These two score highly-trained security personnel were given an added weapon: high-tech armor designed by Tony Stark (creator of the Iron Man armor), and capable of using a wide range of offensive and defensive equipment specifically designed to combat super-powered beings.

When you wore the Guardsman armor, you felt invincible.

Certainly Craig Lynch felt so when he circled Cletus Kasady's containment cell, as was his duty for the hour. It was a boring job usually pulled by the newer guards like Lynch. But he had decided that, since there were no rules against talking to the prisoners, he was going to add a little excitement to his boring job by taunting the prisoner.

So, for the last ten minutes he had leered at Kasady, laughed at him, called him names. With no reaction from Kasady.

Lynch used to play offensive line in college and since then he'd stayed in shape by lifting weights and boxing on weekends. He was a big man, with huge arms, no neck, and powerful shoulders. The gleaming, green Guardsman armor only added to his girth with its three layers of exoskeletal protection. He knew that his size intimidated people, and he used that advantage often. He was not used to having people ignore him as Kasady was doing.

He told anyone who would listen that he didn't fear anyone. And now he especially didn't see why everyone was so afraid of the skinny, wimpy looking redhead in the special containment field.

Craig Lynch certainly wasn't afraid and he was going to prove it.

The room that contained Kasady's jail cell was the size of a small gym. The walls were windowless, except for a high window framed by two machine gun slots. One door in the center of one wall was the only way in or out.

Kasady's actual cell in the center of the large room didn't have the normal steel bars, but instead sheets of high-voltage electric fire on all four sides, under the floor, and above the ceiling. The walls of fire were see-through, like looking though a pink-tinted pane of glass. Except that this "glass" always sparkled and flickered and left a light smell in the room of burning dust, like a heater first turning on after a long summer unused.

Outside of the walls of fire, two Guardsmen were always in the room, one near the door and one walking around the cell. Two more were stationed at the machine gun slots (though what they actually fired were massive flame-throwers) behind three-foot-thick unbreakable glass. Four guards all the time, all with exact orders to shoot first and ask questions later if something happened to the containment cell and Kasady got out.

"So," Lynch said as he continued to slowly circle the fire-walled cell. "You're the clown who supposedly terrorized thousands. With that pathetic skinny body, you're supposed to be the superpowered serial killer Carnage? Are you some kind of a joke or what?"

Kasady only watched from his cot in the center of the floor as the new guard circled him.

Lynch laughed again, still circling. "You just look like another helpless jailbird to me. My mother could take you. And probably would if you weren't so ugly that she wouldn't want to touch you."

Lynch sneered at Kasady and continued circling the cell, doing everything he could to provoke him.

"Lynch," the other guard said from his position near the room's only door. "Go easy with him. Trust me, he's who they say he is."

Again Lynch just laughed and slowly kept circling Kasady.

Kasady followed Lynch's progress with his eyes, but didn't move his body and didn't bother to turn around as Lynch moved behind him. The look on his face showed indifference to Lynch.

"Yeah," Lynch said. "If he's who they say he is, how come he doesn't just step through that firewall an' skag me?"

"I'll bet he wishes he could," the guard beside

the door said in a disgusted tone. "I'm half thinking of doing it myself."

Inside the cell, Kasady made no indication that he agreed one way or the other.

Ignoring the other Guardsman, Lynch stopped directly in front of Kasady. "So how come, tough guy? What's the matter? You afraid of scorchin' your pinkie?"

Kasady's irises were black, intense dots in the center of his large white eyes. Unblinking, he stared at Lynch's sneering face.

"Bet you want to, don't you?" Lynch said. "But you're too scared. Right, Red?"

Slowly Kasady raised his hand and, using the nail on his little finger, scraped a small line on his cheek.

At first it looked like a small black drop of blood trickled down his face toward his chin.

But it wasn't blood.

It was the alien symbiote. The symbiote from another planet that lived inside of Kasady and loved chaos as much, if not more, than he.

Lynch had been briefed about this, but didn't really believe it.

Until now.

Kasady was now Carnage, the greatest and most powerful serial killer of all time.

Like water flowing over his body in all directions, the black and bright red symbiote spread out over Kasady's entire frame, covering his hands in razor-sharp claws, his face with a new face with wide insect eyes, and a huge mouth of long, needle-thin teeth.

Red saliva drooled from that mouth, dripping off those black teeth.

The bright red of blood.

The black of death.

Carnage.

The symbiote didn't stop when it covered Kasady. It seemed to flow, continuously moving and changing, as if a thousand ants were between it and Kasady's skin.

Kasady's thin body seemed to expand under the covering of red and black, growing like a bad dream on a hot, sweaty night.

Carnage stood up, towering over Lynch like an adult over a child.

"Is this what you want, little man?" Carnage's voice seemed to fill the room, godlike in intensity and fullness as if projected through ten speakers.

Lynch stood transfixed, his mouth open, his eyes wide and unblinking, staring at the horror that had grown in front of him. After a moment he tried to swallow, but failed because every ounce of moisture in his throat had dried up.

He took a slight step back.

Carnage slowly raised his hand and pointed all his fingers at Lynch like each was the barrel of a gun, armed and ready to fire. Bloodlike drops ran off those fingers, hitting the floor and merging back with the symbiote in a continuous flow.

Lynch took another step back, raising his arms, preparing to fire the repulsor rays in his gauntlets.

Like fast-motion film of plants growing, Carnage's fingers grew spiked points. The moving symbiote again made the razor-sharp blades look as if blood was already dripping from them.

Lynch's blood.

Lynch took another step back and aimed his gauntlet at the fire-walled cage.

The other guard shouted, "Lynch, don't!"

Carnage fired the spikes from his fingers directly at Lynch like four arrows from a crossbow.

Lynch jumped back again, as if to duck the hurtling death coming at his face, the high-tech weaponry at his disposal completely forgotten.

He tripped and sprawled backward on the smooth floor, his arms raised instinctively over his helmeted face to protect himself.

The spikes hit the fire screen and sparks flew. Blues and oranges and reds lit up the room as the fire-wall vaporized the spikes with a loud hiss.

The fire in the electrical walls surged for a moment, blocking the view of Carnage, and then returned to normal flickering.

The smell of burning sulfur now filled the room.

Carnage stood in the middle of his fire-walled cell and laughed, his voice echoing off the walls, the ceiling, everywhere.

The second guard scrambled around and helped Lynch to his feet.

"Man, you're dumber than you look."

"I just—"

"Don't bother explaining. Just get out of here and send in Frank."

Lynch glanced over at where Carnage stood, laughing. As Lynch half staggered out of the room, Carnage said, "Wimp."

"Try idiot," the other guard said.

Carnage just kept laughing.

CHAPTER 3

The sound of taxis honking and sidewalk construction two blocks down the street woke Peter Parker. The sun was streaming in the open window and he could see blue sky beyond. It seemed, for the moment, that the cold of the upcoming winter was being held back and Manhattan would have one of its notoriously beautiful fall days. Okay, so it wasn't the days he hated about fall. It was the nights. And the promise of winter just around the corner.

Peter stretched slowly under the sheets, working some of the faint soreness out of his muscles from the night.

Beside him, under the soft sheet and thick comforter made by his Aunt May, Mary Jane was also slowly waking up. The sun was directly on her face, making her seem even more beautiful than she was already. Peter studied her square nose, high cheekbones, full lips, and perfect skin. He didn't know how it was possible that she could seem more beautiful, or how he was so fortunate to have someone like her love him. But on this bright fall morning it seemed she was the most beautiful human he could ever imagine.

At times he swore he didn't deserve to be so lucky.

Her long, shiny red hair caught and held the

rays of the sun, the thick strands glowing with a life all their own. Her hair was another thing he just didn't understand. His short brown hair never seemed to do what he wanted it to, no matter how much he combed it, washed it, or even blow-dried it. But somehow her hair always seemed perfect, even waking up like this. Sometimes her hair was so perfect in the morning he felt like he was waking up in a movie.

This morning was one of those mornings. He let his right hand stroke her hair gently, enjoying the silky feel.

Mary Jane slowly opened her deep green eyes and caught him looking at her. She smiled and reached out to touch his cheek gently. "Morning," she whispered.

"Good morning to you."

She snuggled over beside him.

He lay on his back with her head cradled on his shoulder and gazed across the bedroom. He could actually see the beams of early morning sunlight cutting through the light dust in the air. He hadn't used to like waking up in the bright morning light. But since he married Mary Jane she had convinced him it was a nice thing and this morning he agreed with her completely. The natural light off the eggshell-painted walls and brick made the room seem peaceful and that feeling was flooding him. Lately, it was very unusual for him to feel this way.

"You out late last night?" Mary Jane asked as she snuggled her soft and warm hair against Peter and wrapped her leg over his, her silk nightgown feeling smooth and very, very good against his flesh.

But her question brought back what had happened last night with Dr. Catrall, as the government agents had called him. The feeling of comfort and peace disappeared as if a cloud had moved in front of the sun.

"Yeah," Peter said, his gaze on the ceiling. "Got some really stupid shots of the mob guy before he disappeared into this building on Broadway. I sat on a ledge for two hours freezing my butt off waiting for him to come out and he never showed."

"You feel warm now," MJ said, snuggling even closer to him under the heavy quilt.

Peter laughed. "You didn't say that last night when I crawled in. In fact, I remember a few death threats if I got near you with my cold feet."

"Well, a girl's got to protect herself."

He laughed and they snuggled in silence for a few moments.

Then Peter broke the silence. "I did have something weird happen, though. Ran into a couple of government guys following some doctor. Seems they wanted whatever he had in his briefcase."

"And let me guess," she said. "You didn't let them take it. Right?"

"It worked out that way. The doctor seemed almost crazy with fear of those two."

"Any reason why?" Mary Jane asked as she nuzzled against his neck. "Didn't he pay his taxes?"

Peter ignored her second question. "No reason to be that afraid that I could see. You know, now that I think about it, if I got some photos of that guy I might make a little extra from the *Bugle*." He moved away from Mary Jane to get dressed, his mind on figuring out a way to find Dr. Catrall and discover what was going on.

But Mary Jane didn't want to let him go. She kept her arm around his neck, kissing him playfully. "You know," she said, "you don't have to be in class at the university until this afternoon. And since I lost the soap opera job, I sure don't have to get up."

"But MJ, if I can find that guy we could sure use the extra money." He untangled himself from her and stood, searching the floor for where he dropped his pants.

Behind him, Mary Jane turned away from him and covered herself with the quilt. Peter, even without his spider-sense, could tell he had goofed. Big time husband goof. Sometimes he was about as sensitive as a doorjamb.

Mary Jane had always been an extremely independent woman. Without the acting job on the soap opera, she wasn't carrying her own weight on the money side of their relationship. Their marriage, right from the start, had been based on being a true partnership. Now, she was extremely down about not having a job. It wasn't as if she wasn't trying. She was, and she would be working again soon. Peter knew that without a doubt.

But she didn't believe him when he reassured her. And he supposed that if the tables were turned, he wouldn't believe her, either. Sort of a nature-of-the-beast kind of thing.

At least he could try to be a little more sensitive.

He stared at her quilt-covered back for a long moment. He didn't have a clue how to help her with her self-esteem problems. He would just be there for her where and when he could. She would have to regain the rest on her own.

But he could at least take her mind off of her problems for a short time.

And enjoy it in the process.

He crawled back into bed and snuggled up against her back, nuzzling at her neck through her soft red hair.

"Thought you were in a hurry?" she said, her voice muffled in her pillow.

"Decided I had some extra time after all this morning. I'm sure I remember Jonah, Robbie, and Kate having some sort of meeting or something."

Mary Jane snorted. "You want me to believe that line?"

"I sure hope so." He snuggled closer with his body and she laughed. "Besides, I can't think of anyone in the world I would rather spend time with than my beautiful wife."

She laughed softly again as he snuggled up tight against her back and pressed his face into her soft hair. It smelled of fresh peaches and clean air. A Mary Jane smell. He loved it. How she managed that in New York he would never know, but she always did.

Slowly her shoulders relaxed and she turned to face him. "Peter Parker, you sure have a way with *words.*"

He pulled her tight against him. "Let's hope that's not all I have a way with."

"Yeah," she said, laughing. "Let's hope."

And then she kissed him.

An hour later Peter had just slipped into his Spider-Man suit and had the mask in his hand. He figured it would be a lot faster to web his way uptown than catch a subway. He didn't know where to start looking for Dr. Catrall, but he imagined he'd find a place at the *Daily Bugle.*

Mary Jane crawled out of bed and slipped into

her robe as Peter stared appreciatively.

"What are you looking at?" she asked, smiling.

"Lady, if you don't know by now, you're in big trouble."

She laughed and then the smile dropped from her face. "Peter, you be careful with these government types." She moved up to him, kissed him, then hugged him hard.

"They're the FBI, not the IRS, so there's no need to worry. Besides, this pair doesn't have a brain cell between them."

"Just play it safe anyway," she said. Then she kissed him hard again.

After a long moment she finally released him. "Wow," he said. "I might have to make sure all my classes next semester are afternoon classes."

"By then I'll be working and you'll be out of luck."

"Well then, what do you say that this semester I just skip a few classes?"

She laughed and punched his arm playfully.

He loved times like this with Mary Jane. Too bad there couldn't be more of them.

He slipped on his mask and eased toward the window, staying out of sight of anyone in nearby buildings. His spider-sense told him it was clear, that no one was watching him, so with a wave to Mary Jane he hit the neighboring building with a web and swung out over the street.

* * *

Mary Jane stood back from the window and watched as her husband swung out of sight. Then smiling, she turned and headed for the kitchen to start her coffee.

It had been really nice of Peter to stay and help cheer her up. But there really wasn't anything he could do beyond taking her mind off the problem of not working. And that he was very good at, both with fun hours like this morning and making her worry about him in his fights as Spider-Man. She had known what she was getting into when they got married, but sometimes she just wished he would slow down a little.

Of course, she wagered that many wives wished the very same of their husbands at one time or another.

And husbands thought as much of their working wives. She knew Peter had said to slow down a few times when she was working so hard on the soap opera.

Of course, that was now gone. It was time she found something new.

She had just started her coffee and was about to head back to the bedroom to get ready for the day's job search when the doorbell rang.

Through the peephole she could see the top of May Parker's head, Peter's elderly aunt.

Mary Jane quickly opened the door.

"Aunt May. What a pleasant surprise. Come in."

Aunt May was wearing her brown, fall cloth coat and a cloth hat over her fine gray hair. She had a matching brown, oversized handbag over one arm and was wringing her hands together in a fashion that Mary Jane immediately knew meant problems.

Aunt May nodded to Mary Jane and said hello, but didn't smile. She stepped into the apartment and quickly glanced around. "Is Peter in? It seems that I—I'm in, well . . ." She stammered for a moment, her face red.

Then she turned to face Mary Jane and blurted it out. "I'm in a bit of trouble."

CHAPTER 4

The controlled but constant pandemonium of the *Daily Bugle* newsroom always got Peter's blood stirring, just like a good fight as Spider-Man did.

The room was huge, with a fairly low ceiling, lots of bright fluorescent lights, and square columns every twenty feet. A maze of pathways, file cabinets, and desks filled every inch of the room between the thick columns, like a thousand giant children's blocks scattered in no particular fashion.

Paper seemed to cover every exposed surface as if it had snowed the night before.

Glassed-in offices lined the far wall of the room where the senior editors and publisher did their jobs. At the end, to the right of the main door, were glass conference rooms and at the other end was a huge meeting room without windows.

At ten in the morning a good fifty people filled the big room, some sitting at desks pounding on keyboards and staring at computer monitors. Others were hurrying from one place to another, fighting their way through the maze, papers clutched in their hands. Still others stood in groups talking, hands moving to emphasize their points.

Phones constantly rang.

People constantly shouted.

Printers spit out continuous reams of paper.

This morning, even though the fall day was still cool, the big newsroom felt slightly hot and smelled of ink and excitement.

It was a catching smell, one that filled any visitor's blood instantly. It was impossible to walk slowly through the big room.

The dull roar of the room always hit new arrivals like a hammer to the face as they opened the swinging doors from the elevator lobby. Peter had never got used to that feeling. Granted, the streets of New York were loud, but nothing like the *Daily Bugle* newsroom at ten in the morning.

Every morning.

Seven days a week.

Peter stepped inside and let the doors swing shut behind him as the noise and excitement flooded over and around him. He loved this place, almost as much as the science labs at the university.

With a glance around, he saw what he was looking for and, in ten quick steps around two desks and a quick duck behind a file cabinet, he had snagged the arm of Danny, a freshman intern, as he scampered past.

The kid had red hair, brown eyes, and more freckles than anyone could count. He was carrying two notebooks full of paper and, like everyone else in the room, looked to be in a massive hurry.

"I need some help," Peter said.

At that very moment J. Jonah Jameson, the *Bugle*'s publisher, saw Peter from across the room and indicated with a wave that Peter should join him in the big conference room.

Peter nodded and indicated that he would do just that, then turned to Danny.

"Darn it, Peter," Danny said before Peter could even open his mouth. "Thomson's got me running my legs off on her current project with the waterworks. She wants me to dig twenty files out of the morgue and have them back to her in one hour. One hour! Can you imagine anyone doing twenty files in one hour? That woman never seems to stop and I—"

"I need information on a Dr. Catrall," Peter said, ignoring Danny as if he wasn't even talking. "See what you can find for me as quick as you can. I'll be with good old Jonah in the conference room, so don't be too long on it."

He patted Danny on the arm and turned away before the poor kid could object any more.

Peter smiled, pleased with himself. So many people had done that to him in his early days around the *Bugle* that he had the technique down to a science now. No one around a newspaper ever had enough time and if you waited until someone did, you'd never get any help. That had been a hard lesson for Peter to learn those first years. But he had learned it well.

He threaded his way through the desks, saying hello to people as he went, until he reached the door on the side where Jonah had disappeared.

Normally the big double doors to the conference room were closed, but this morning they stood wide open. The room was generally used for large staff meetings and Christmas parties. Day after day it sat dark and empty, the place where whispered meetings were held while standing in the shadows. Over the years Peter had had a number of those whisper-meetings in the dark conference room.

But now the lights were all turned up bright and there were at least twenty television monitors set up on desks and tables around the room. Most were turned off, but two technicians were working on one, and a few others were turned on to show a large area of what looked like Central Park via a direct-link camera feed.

Jonah was standing in the middle of the room talking to a reporter named Joy Mercado. She was a tall, lithe blonde who looked like an ordinary businesswoman at first glance. Once she started talking, though, you realized how formidable she could be. Her mind was always about ten steps ahead of her mouth and about twenty steps ahead of whoever she was talking to. Even with his enhanced strength and speed, he always had a hard time keeping up with Joy.

J. Jonah Jameson, on the other hand, was a large, middle-aged sort, with a square jaw and flat-top hair cut. Normally, he had a big, smelly cigar stuck in one corner of his mouth and he never talked in a normal voice, but preferred, it seemed, to yell. He was as self-centered as they came and ran the newspaper like the cheapest miser imaginable. Despite the gruff facade and Scrooge-like penny-pinching, however, Jonah was also one of the best newspapermen in the business, with an unsurpassable passion for his work.

"Well, Parker," Jonah called out, pulling the cigar out of his mouth to shout. "What do you think of my new media room?" Jonah swept his cigar around in a grand gesture that indicated that Peter should look at all of the room and Peter did as he was told.

It never hurt to humor the publisher. Especially when Peter was looking to sell him pictures.

"Impressive," Peter said. "What's it for?"

"To watch the worldwide coverage of Feed 'Em All," Jonah said, sounding half-disgusted that Peter would have to ask. "Every monitor will be hooked to a different satellite feed from around the world. I want to watch them all. Great idea, huh?"

"That it is," Peter said, taking in the room

again. Feed 'Em All was an event being sponsored by the *Daily Bugle.* The idea behind it was to give every homeless person in New York one good meal. Jonah had somehow managed to get businesses from around the city to donate the materials and a half dozen large trailers had been parked on the roadway alongside Belvedere Lake, adjacent to the great lawn in Central Park.

What seemed to be a half-mile of tables had been set up, with a long one nearest the trailers as the food serving center. A dozen big pots were being used to create great quantities of stew and a dozen more pots were lined up on the tables for cooking vegetables. Portable ovens were lined along the trailers and hooked up to generators for heating bread. It looked like it was going to be quite a feast.

Jonah, in a memo to everyone a few weeks earlier, had stated that the goals of this project were to raise awareness of the homeless problem, both in New York and around the world, and to spur common people to be just as generous as he was being.

Peter just hoped the homeless decided to show up and he knew without a doubt there would be no "common" people there; only the rich wanting to be *seen* at this event.

Peter also hoped that no one pointed out to Jonah that the homeless shelters all over the city did the same thing Jonah and the *Bugle* were doing in Central Park. Only they did it twice a day, every day of the year, and never received worldwide publicity for doing it.

"Parker," Jonah said, "I want you to get some shots of this room. And of course, cover the event itself. We can use all the photos we can get of this."

"Will do, Boss," Peter said. Good. That would help the financial situation out a little.

One of the technicians banged one monitor and Jonah yelled at him, then headed that way, leaving Joy and Peter alone.

Peter shook his head as he watched his boss storm across the room.

Beside him Joy laughed. "This is going to be a huge publicity scoop for Jonah." Then she added sarcastically, "I wonder if he realizes that?"

It was Peter's turn to laugh. "Only if it works," he said.

Joy glanced at him. "You got that right."

"Peter!" Danny called for him from the door. In his hand was a computer printout.

"See ya," Peter said to Joy and headed for Danny. They met halfway across the media room and Danny handed him the printout, then, without a word, turned and almost ran for the clutter and crowded desks of the newsroom.

Peter smiled at the kid's departing back. He was

learning quickly. Another few months and Peter would have to find another intern to help him.

Peter strolled slowly toward the newsroom, reading the printout as he went.

It seemed that Dr. Eric Catrall was a prominent genetic engineer currently employed by a private firm called Lifestream Technologies. Catrall was responsible for several advancements in DNA research and was considered one of the world's leading experts in the unraveling of genetic codes.

"So what were you doing in that alley in the middle of the night?" Peter muttered aloud.

"Talking to yourself again, Parker?"

Peter looked up into the face of Ben Urich, who stood in the doorway to the newsroom. Ben was one of the *Bugle*'s top investigative reporters. He was a lanky man, standing over six feet tall, with huge hands and a laconic, disarming smile. Ben had helped both Spider-Man and Peter Parker a number of times over the years and Peter respected the man a great deal.

"I'm the only one who will listen around here," Peter said as he folded up the printout and put it in his pocket.

Ben laughed. "I know that feeling. Say, you got some fresh photos of Carnage tucked away at home?"

"Carnage?" Peter asked, a knot snapping his stomach tight and making his throat instantly dry.

His stomach twisted every time Carnage's name was mentioned, but this time it seemed worse.

"Yeah, good old Carnage," Ben said. "Come on, Peter. You wouldn't happen to have a few photos you're holding out for a sequel to *Webs*?"

Peter smiled and shook his head. *Webs* was a coffee-table book of Peter's Spider-Man photos. It did well, and could still be found in the photography section of larger bookstores. The periodic royalty checks came in handy these days, too. Still, there were no present plans for a sequel, and even if there were, he wouldn't hold back pictures he could get more immediate cash for.

Peter asked, "I thought Carnage was old news. Isn't Cletus Kasady still locked up tight out in Colorado?"

When Ben glanced around to make sure no one was listening to what he was about to say, Peter felt the knot tighten. Carnage was one of the worst foes Spider-Man had ever faced. Carnage had killed more people than Peter ever wanted to count and Peter felt responsible for every death.

"They're transferring Carnage from the Vault. They're doing some experiments on Kasady, to try to neutralize his whacked-out body chemistry. They figure they might be able to kill Carnage without killing Kasady."

"You're kidding?"

Ben shook his head. Peter could tell he was excited by the story.

But Peter wasn't excited. The more Ben told him the more his stomach twisted.

"The authorities have been keeping this real hush-hush," Ben said. "They don't want to stir up public fear and protest. But I got hold of the details."

Peter took a deep breath and asked the question to which he was most afraid of answer. "Where are they taking him? For the experiments, that is."

Ben glanced around again, but no one was close to them at the edge of the newsroom, so he pulled out a proof sheet of his story from an inside pocket and handed it to Peter.

"Cover of the afternoon edition."

Peter's hands shook as he held the *Bugle* front page with the headline roughly blocked in.

CARNAGE IN NEW YORK!

CHAPTER 5

When the big, old brick and stone Brooklyn school just across the river from Manhattan was first built, it was used as a grade school. The laughter of children playing on the open playground on warm fall afternoons would fill the neighborhood like music filled concert halls. Generations of children learned how to read and write in those high-ceilinged rooms.

It was a building of laughter and warmth and learning for over thirty years.

Then, in the early sixties, extra classrooms were added onto the school, a parking lot was poured over the old playground, a huge gym was built on the ground floor, and the grade school became a high school.

For the next twenty years the sounds of laughter came not from young innocent children, but from young lovers getting to know each other between classes.

Or friends planning the night out.

Or fans talking about the latest win of their basketball team.

The old school continued to be a place where children and young adults learned and memories were made.

But in the late eighties the school became too old and expensive to maintain. Its time had passed and, against the objections of the older families in the surrounding neighborhood, the city sold it to a private firm that someday hoped to convert it to offices.

For the eight years since the sale the grand old school had sat abandoned and unused, children of its former students breaking out its windows with rocks and writing crude sayings on its walls with spray cans.

But now, the school had found another purpose and for a day or so it had come back to life.

A very different life from teaching and providing wisdom and joy to children. This time the old building came back to life to kill something.

All the old echoes of laughter were gone from the building now. The gymnasium had been converted into an armed fortress. The huge room that once held the cheers from grandstands full of parents and students now contained enough firepower to defeat most small countries' armies.

Just as the attention of the cheering fans had been directed to the middle of the room, so were all the guns, all the modern defensive machines, all the weapons of destruction. All aimed at the very center of the old wood-floored room in a pattern of deadly crossfire.

For the moment, that center was empty.

Fiorello, the captain of the hundred-strong heavily armed force, was a short, stocky man who always wore a Mets baseball cap and a light brown jacket over a tee-shirt. He had a .357 Magnum strapped to his waist just inside his jacket in an easily reachable position and obvious to anyone who approached him. He liked it that way. In his line of work—guarding the most dangerous humans in the world—he needed every bit of respect from everyone around him. That respect some day might save some of his people's lives.

He was studying all the gun emplacements for the second time, lining up each weapon—flame-throwers to capitalize on Carnage's main weakness of intense heat—and setting firing limits to make sure the shooters weren't barbecuing each other across the room, when a sound drew his attention.

On the far side of the gym, double doors were tossed open and his second-in-command entered the room and signaled to him that it was time.

He nodded that it was clear to start and a moment later three armed guards stepped through where years before basketball teams used to burst into the gym to the cheers of the crowds.

But this time the opening of those doors sent no cheers rattling in the wooden rafters; instead, the room fell into a deathly silence.

Fiorello watched, making sure every detail went as he had planned.

Five guards took up positions along the wall

near the door, their weapons held in a ready position.

"Everyone get set!" Fiorello shouted at the room. "All weapons up and armed!"

Around the room a faint clicking echoed off the old wooden rafters and the shiny new, high tech equipment that the scientists had installed.

Through the wide doors a box of fire was pushed smoothly onto the gym floor. It was a box no bigger than a small bedroom, about ten feet square and eight feet high. It had a wide metal base on ten solid rubber wheels. The walls were electrical fields that formed a flickering fire barrier that would instantly burn anything that touched it.

The box of fire held a very dangerous man.

Carnage.

Trailing from the box were three huge reinforced cables hooked up to two massive portable generators.

Fiorello knew that if one failed, the other would have enough power to maintain the electrical fire walls. Another generating unit inside the base of the cell would maintain the walls for one minute even with both generators down or the wires cut.

Every precaution that he and others could think of had been taken for this move. And he still didn't like it.

Not one bit.

Inside the walls of electrical fire stood Cletus Kasady, dressed in a standard Vault prison uniform. He braced himself against a chair. His red hair looked even redder through the flickering fire walls. He studied the gym and all the guns and machines in an unhurried fashion, the expression on his face almost one of laughter. He was the greatest serial killer of all time and the most feared. He seemed to be enjoying the fear he saw around him and all the problems and attention he caused.

A total of twenty Guardsmen that had traveled with him from Colorado took up their new positions around the gym, looking properly fearsome in their green, featureless armor. The box of fire was rolled into the center of the gym floor.

One hundred and twenty against one. Fiorello hoped that would be enough if something happened. He doubted it would be.

Carnage was here.

Fiorello watched as more of his people trained their high-powered flamethrowers on the cell and others primed the lasers and sound cannons. If something went wrong Kasady would find himself in the middle of the worst hell he could imagine.

Fiorello nodded to himself. So far so good, but it had just started. Anything could go wrong.

He strolled across the wooden floor and up to the box of fire. First he checked the generators and let the operators standing next to each one assure him they were all running fine. Then he studied the base of the cell carefully, walking all the way around it, checking every detail.

Fiorello considered himself a man of principles, but he hated this assignment. If it had been up to him he would have just ordered his men to open fire on Carnage, or Kasady, or whatever he was called, and just get this over with. Better for society and much safer.

But it wasn't up to him, as he had been told, so he did his job. His job was to make sure at all costs that Carnage didn't escape.

"See anything you like?" Kasady asked as he sat down on the cell's only chair.

Fiorello glanced up into the dark black holes of Kasady's eyes. "Yeah," Fiorello said. "I see that you're not going anywhere except straight to hell."

Fiorello turned and signaled to a man named O'Keefe that he could start getting his equipment ready.

O'Keefe was the chief scientist on this experiment. He was a tall guy, with almost no hair and big, bottle-thick glasses. Like the rest of the scientists and lab techs with him, he was dressed in a white lab coat. The visible armed guards outnumbered the scientists at least three to one.

Fiorello turned back to Kasady. "Pretty soon you'll just be another loser in a cell on Ryker's

Island. Now aren't you going to enjoy that?"

"Killing you is what I'm going to enjoy," Kasady said.

Fiorello snorted and pointed around him at all the weapons aimed at Kasady. "Well, Red, you can just tell I'm trembling in my boots."

"If you weren't trembling, Fiorello," Kasady said, "you wouldn't have so many guns aimed at me."

Fiorello turned his back on Kasady and headed for where O'Keefe was working. All the way across the gym floor he could feel Kasady's gaze boring into his back.

"Doc, this damn well better work," Fiorello said quietly to O'Keefe.

Without looking up, O'Keefe said, "Don't worry. Carnage will be history before the day is out. And then you can do whatever you want with Kasady."

Fiorello glanced around to where Kasady was still staring at him. "I sure hope you're right."

Spider-Man didn't notice the beautiful fall day that filled the canyons between the buildings of Manhattan with sunshine and clean air. He had left the *Bugle* office and changed into costume. Now he webbed from building to building, heading home, his thoughts gloomy and only on Carnage.

He knew the route between the *Bugle* offices and his Upper East Side apartment by heart, every building, every swing around a corner. Even though he was swinging hundreds of feet above the city streets, his mind kept wandering back to the days when Carnage had been created.

It had been partly his own fault, and he still blamed himself, to some degree, for the existence of both Carnage and Venom. If he'd just left the symbiote on the Beyonder's World a lot of innocent people would still be alive.

His web hit the perfect spot on the next building and he swung out through the clear, crisp air, his mind ignoring the busy street below him and wandering back to the time on the Beyonder's World.

He and several other super heroes and super-villains had been brought to a patchwork alien world as a sort of good-guy-vs.-bad-guy contest by a powerful being called the Beyonder. At one point, his costume had been fairly well shredded, and he was looking to repair it. Two fellow heroes had found a place to repair their own costumes, and he went to where they directed him.

It looked like a giant laboratory. On a table was what looked like a small black ball. When he approached the ball, the ball changed. In a lightning-quick motion it had covered his arm and then his entire body. It was like a black, skin-tight sheath that he could put on or take off with but a thought.

The perfect costume, and that was all he thought it was. Nothing more; just another costume.

Even after the new suit had helped him win the fight on the Beyonder's World, he still thought of it as little more than a snappier set of duds. So he brought it back to Earth with him.

That was his big mistake.

Back on Earth, with the help of Reed Richards of the Fantastic Four, Peter discovered that the costume was actually a living alien symbiote and that it was attempting to permanently bond with him.

Panicked at the thought of being linked for life with an alien he didn't understand, Peter tried to destroy it by subjecting it to the intense sound of a church bell. Loud noises and fire were among the alien's few weaknesses.

Unfortunately, the creature was only weakened by the attack. When it revived, it was very angry at Peter that he had rejected it. Very angry indeed.

So it looked around for a new host.

And it found Eddie Brock, a man who hated Spider-Man as much as the symbiote now did.

The two joined and formed a slaughter-minded monster called Venom.

And people started dying.

In a huge battle among Spidey and Venom and

the villains, Styx and Stone, Styx touched Venom with his withering, cancerous touch and seemingly sent the symbiote to its death.

But this symbiote was proving very hard to kill.

Eddie Brock, saved from Styx's deadly touch by the symbiote, was jailed. His cellmate turned out to be the unrepentant, sociopathic serial killer named Cletus Kasady.

When the symbiote recovered, it found Eddie again and rejoined him.

Together, no regular prison could hold them and they escaped. But in the escape Venom left behind a little surprise on the bars of the cell.

A seed.

A spawn.

A hate-child that went in search of its own human host and found Kasady.

Kasady welcomed the symbiote and the two joined forever. In return for the joining, the symbiote gave Kasady horrible powers even beyond Venom's.

Powers to kill.

The joining mutated Kasady's blood and now, unlike Venom, they could never be separated. With that mutation, the link between Kasady and the symbiote formed the worst killing machine ever imagined: Carnage.

Kasady, before the joining, had worshipped chaos like a religion. He loved the freedom expressed by random acts of violence and he lived by that belief, killing at will and without remorse. He wanted to teach the world that anybody can kill any person at any time for any reason. He believed that would bring the world true freedom.

Kasady had no conscience. He would kill, without reason or provocation, as had always been his goal.

With the symbiote and the forming of Carnage, Kasady now had the power to carry out that goal.

Hundreds had died.

Spider-Man shook his head to clear away the graveyard of faces floating before his eyes.

He took a few deep breaths of the crisp air and let the rays of the sun warm him for a moment.

That helped.

The faces faded and were gone. At least for now.

He took another deep breath. He shouldn't be thinking like that. It did no good and he knew it. He had always learned to take responsibility for his actions but he was having a problem with this one.

He felt deep down inside that Carnage was his problem and his fault, no matter how much he tried to force himself to think otherwise.

So he had to be there this afternoon when Carnage "died."

Spider-Man had to be there to make sure.

He studied the window of his apartment and his spider-sense told him no one was watching, but that someone was in the apartment with Mary Jane.

I wonder who that could be? he thought as he swung down to the street and did a quick change in the alley.

Then he ran up the front stairs and let himself in the front door of their apartment.

Aunt May and Mary Jane were both sitting at the kitchen table sipping coffee. They looked up and smiled at Peter when he came through the door.

"Hi, Aunt May," Peter said. "Glad to see you."

And he really was.

It would be nice to take his mind off the problems of Carnage by visiting with the woman who had raised him. She was always so positive and up about things. He could feel his mood lifting as he walked across the room toward her.

Aunt May let Peter give her a quick peck on the cheek and then waited until he had kissed Mary Jane and dropped into the chair across the table from her.

"Go ahead, May," Mary Jane said, putting her hand on Aunt May's.

Peter felt the ease drain from his shoulders to be replaced with tension. "Something wrong?"

Aunt May, for a moment, had trouble meeting

Peter's gaze. Then she finally looked at him and he knew he was right. Something was very wrong.

"Peter," she said softly, seemingly trying to get some courage up. "You know how I hate to involve family with problems, but there just doesn't seem to be anything more I can do."

"Whatever you want, Aunt May," Peter said, glancing at Mary Jane who was nodding in agreement. "All you have to do is ask. You know that."

And Peter meant it. There was no telling what his life would have been like without the caring and understanding of this woman. He truly would do anything in his, or Spider-Man's, power for her.

"Well," Aunt May said, "I hope you can help. You see, I'm about to lose my house."

"What?" Peter said, glancing at Mary Jane to confirm what he had just heard.

Mary Jane just nodded.

It was true.

CHAPTER 6

The smell of bacon in the greasy spoon diner filled Dr. Catrall's nose with a sense of peace and memories of his mother's wonderful Sunday breakfasts, while at the same time making him even hungrier than he already was. And since he hadn't eaten in almost thirty-six hours, that was very, very hungry.

He let the front door of the diner swing closed behind him and shut off the noise of the street and the city. Then he stood near the door and studied the place, afraid that he would find police or FBI agents staring back at him.

Ten people in the diner and no one looked up. Not even the waitress talking to three women near the back.

It was a typical New York City diner. Long and narrow, almost like a train car. The room disappeared back into the depths of the larger building, with, Dr. Catrall hoped, a back door leading out into an alley.

A counter ran down the left side, and vinyl-covered stools sprouted out of the scarred tile in front of the counter like mushrooms on a forest floor. A long mirror behind the shelves of glasses and coffee cups helped make the room look wider than it actually was.

Metal booths lined the right wall, with backs

just tall enough to ensure some privacy, but not tall enough to hide in. Coat hooks stuck out slightly into the aisle from the top of each booth, and pictures of meadows and snow-capped mountains hung on the brick wall.

On each booth table was a large jar of sugar, a bottle of ketchup, and plastic salt and pepper shakers. Plastic-coated menus were stuck against the wall behind the sugar. The kitchen seemed to be at the back on the counter side.

At this time of the morning, after the breakfast rush but before lunch, there were only a few customers: no one Dr. Catrall recognized and no one that looked suspicious enough to work for the government.

After his close call last night he was taking very few chances.

He slipped into the second booth on the side facing the front and carefully placed the briefcase on the seat between him and the wall. If someone did come in he would make a run for it toward the back. He just hoped there was a back door out through the kitchen. If there wasn't, he was as trapped as he had been last night.

A waitress with short blonde hair and a name tag that read *Constance* walked over holding a pot of coffee and an empty cup. She smiled at him with concern in her eyes.

"You look like you could use this," she said as she slipped the cup on the table.

"Oh, yes," Dr. Catrall said. "Thanks a lot."

He had spent the night huddled in a doorway at the bottom of a stairwell. The stairs had led down into the basement of an empty building that had been abandoned for what must have been years. Kids and the homeless had used the stairwell for a bathroom more times than he wanted to think about and the smell had made his stomach upset for most of the night.

He had managed to stay close to the boarded up door and just out of the rain, but not much more than that. He couldn't remember when he had been that cold before.

He had huddled down there and just thought. Thoughts of his work, of his ex-wife, of a warm bed. It was only hunger this morning that drove him out of that doorway and up those steps to take a chance at finding a safe place to eat.

She poured the coffee and then stepped back. "Anything else?"

He glanced up at her. If he had had a daughter, she would be about Constance's age. But he didn't have a daughter or a son. And his wife had left him years before. His entire life had been his work and now that too was gone.

He had nothing.

His life was over.

"You all right, Mister?" Constance asked. Her smile was now totally gone and she showed real concern.

Dr. Catrall shook his head back and forth to clear it. "Just had a long night," he said. "Working way too hard." He patted the briefcase resting on the seat between him and the wall.

He'd bought a newspaper from the vendor outside and he now moved the paper over and rested it on the briefcase. "I could use some breakfast. You have any of that bacon left that I can smell?"

"Sure do," she said, pulling out her pad and pencil. "Eggs and toast, too?"

"That would be wonderful," he said. "Over-easy."

"Won't be too long." She turned and headed back for the kitchen and he put both hands around the hot coffee cup trying to get some heat into them again.

How had he come this far?

How did he end up like this, afraid of every shadow, hiding in empty buildings?

What had happened to his life?

For years he'd been doing good work, rewarding work, for Lifestream Technologies. He'd been searching for the DNA strand responsible for violent behavior in humans. If he had succeeded, his work would have been used in formulating a cure for psychoses of all types.

He would have won the Nobel and it would have made him rich beyond his wildest dreams.

Now those dreams turned out to be nothing but wild nightmares.

He had failed.

It was that simple.

Before he could locate the specific strand of DNA, he had discovered something else. Something that, at the time, he only considered a great signpost, letting him know he was on the right track. His discovery was a catalyst, a golden liquid compound that could *activate* the violence trigger in otherwise normal people.

A golden liquid that, with a simple touch, would make a peaceful, perfectly sane person go crazy and kill anything in his or her path.

The very opposite of what he had been spending his life working toward.

He laughed to himself softly and sipped his coffee, letting the hot liquid work to warm his insides. That day, just a little less than a year ago now, had been so great. It had been the first big breakthrough, and he and his staff were certain it would lead to what they were searching for.

And he supposed, given enough time, it would have. But he wasn't given the time.

Four months after the discovery of the "trigger," as he liked to call it, he accidentally discovered his work was being monitored beyond normal channels. For two months he trusted no one while doing a subtle investigation on his own. What he had discovered had shocked him to his very core.

Lifestream Technologies had ties with covert government agencies, as well as regular ones, such as the FBI and CIA. Much of Lifestream's funding came from the covert sources.

Much of *his* funding.

And worst of all, his "trigger" that had been such good news months before was being considered for battlefield applications and covert operations.

He'd been slipped a study of one covert plan where the CIA, using his discovery, put his "trigger" into the water supply of a hostile country and then stood back while the people of that country destroyed each other.

The study showed a sixty percent kill rate in a country where his discovery would be put through the major water supplies.

Millions dead if they used it. And he knew the military mind. Given the chance, they *would* use it.

No one cared that he was working to end violence. Instead they were going to use his accidental discovery to kill even more people.

Millions and millions of people.

That he couldn't stand for.

He'd stolen the only existing sample of the "trigger" and ran. The notes he'd left behind were worthless. Catrall was eidetic, only taking notes when reminded, and his staff had long since given up reminding him. To get his secret they needed to have him. Or his only sample.

So he'd run with the sample.

That had been five days ago.

He still didn't know what to do with it.

He couldn't pour it out because it was so powerful that even a microscopic fraction of a drop in the water system or the ground water or the river would be devastating for the city and maybe even the surrounding state. He didn't know for sure if it would work that way, but he didn't dare take the chance.

And he was carrying a complete vial full of the fluid.

More than enough to drive every man, woman, and child in the entire United States crazy with violence.

If it had broken last night when he brushed it against the railing it might have washed into the sewers and then down into the eco-system. It didn't dilute. It took decades to degrade to a harmless level. It couldn't be filtered out of water by any known working process.

It was pure death.

Actually, much worse than simple death. It

turned whoever touched it into a violent killing machine by altering their very DNA structure. Not only was it death for the person who touched it, but it was death for anyone around that person.

Now that he was seeing clearly he could understand why the government wanted it.

And he wasn't going to let them have it.

The wonderful smell of bacon and toast flooded his senses and brought him back to the present problem. That of getting some food and some energy to move on and keep hiding.

Constance slipped the plate onto the table in front of him and smiled. "More coffee?"

He pushed his cup forward, his hand slightly shaking. "Please."

She poured and then turned to wait on a couple near the back. He watched her for a moment, wondering why he had made the choices in his life that he had. He should have taken the job at the university, taught two classes per week, and had a family like his ex-wife Bridget wanted him to do. But no, he had had higher goals.

He was going to save humanity from itself.

Stupid goals, Bridget had called them the day she left him. Goals driven in him by the insanity of his father. Insanity that he had nightmares about year after year.

Maybe Bridget had been right. Maybe what he had needed wasn't his work, but counseling.

He took a deep breath and dug into the breakfast in front of him.

He had finished all three pieces of bacon, both eggs, and two of the four slices of toast when a heavy hand dropped onto his shoulder.

He spun around and saw two men in business suits. One man had his suit slightly open and Dr. Catrall could see the butt of his gun.

They both stood in the aisle between the booth and the counter.

"You got away from the Seek Team last night, Doc," the guy closest to him said. "Thanks to Spider-Man. But we're all over the city. It was only a matter of time."

Dr. Catrall panicked.

He wanted to scream, to lash out, to fight.

They were going to take his discovery and use it to hurt people.

He couldn't let that happen.

Grabbing the handle of the briefcase with his left hand he swung it up and around hard, hitting the agent standing in the aisle closest to him squarely in the stomach.

He felt the agent grab at the case, so he yanked it back.

The guy let out a huge breath, then doubled over gasping for air.

With the briefcase in his hand, Dr. Catrall slid to the edge of his seat. But before he could stand the other man was on him like a bulldozer pushing dirt.

He shoved Dr. Catrall down hard into the booth and, with a vicious backhand, slapped the doctor hard across the side of the head.

The almost-empty plate clattered against the brick wall and his fork fell to the floor.

Dr. Catrall's ears were ringing and the side of his face where the man had hit him ached. He could taste blood and a tooth felt loose.

But he didn't care.

He had to get away or die trying. He couldn't live with the knowledge of what they would do with his work. He couldn't live with the thought that he had killed millions of people.

He leaped back up at the man just as a deep voice shouted, "Hold it right there! All of you!"

Dr. Catrall froze.

The man kneeling on the floor trying to catch his breath looked up, and the guy that had hit Catrall glanced over his shoulder, right into the double barrels of a shotgun held by a big man in a white apron. Constance stood behind him with a worried look on her face.

Dr. Catrall stayed still, not knowing what to do next.

The big man with the shotgun was very heavy-set, with a bald head and bushy eyebrows. He had on a stained apron that said, *Because I own the place, that's why!*

He also looked as if he knew exactly what to do with the shotgun and wasn't afraid to do it.

"You know," the diner's owner said, "I've come to expect violence in this part of town. Kinda goes with the neighborhood, if you know what I mean."

"Let me explain," the guy kneeling managed to get out between breaths. "Let me show you—"

"You reach into that pocket and I will guarantee you a closed-casket funeral," the owner said. "And I don't really care who you are."

The government agent froze.

"I have this policy around here," the owner said, nodding and smiling at the frozen men facing his gun. "I like to help the underdog."

"But—" A quick movement of the barrel of the shotgun cut off the agent's remark.

"Now, since there's two of you and only one of him, I suppose that makes him the underdog, doesn't it? So get going." The guy waved the gun barrel at the front door and nodded to the doctor.

Dr. Catrall moved quickly, pulling the briefcase off the table, grabbing the newspaper, and standing. He quickly slid past the agents and headed for the door, then suddenly stopped.

"Forgot to pay for breakfast," he said. He turned and slapped a ten and a five on the counter top. "Keep the rest as a tip. And thanks."

The owner of the diner smiled at him and Constance nodded, the look of worry still on her face.

A subway train entrance sat right outside the diner, which was part of the reason why Catrall chose this particular place to eat. The doctor ran down the metal-tipped steps. As he fumbled for a token, he heard two sounds: the footfalls of the agents running down the stairs behind him, and the rumble of an arriving 9 train. He put in his token, ran into the open doors, and sighed with great relief as the doors closed behind him.

As the train pulled out, he could see the agents on the platform, swearing.

Mary Jane handed Peter a hot cup of coffee as he sat across the kitchen table from his Aunt May. "Thanks," he said and sipped it, trying to push the thoughts of Carnage out of his mind so he could listen clearly to his Aunt's story.

MJ had opened the blinds on all the windows and sunlight flooded the apartment, making it feel lighter and bigger than it really was. He loved this place and he loved how MJ had made it feel like a home.

"I'm really sorry for bringing you children into this," Aunt May said, her voice hesitant. "But I just don't have any more ideas."

Peter couldn't remember the last time he had seen his aunt this upset and worried.

"Aunt May," Peter said, touching her hand across the table, "just tell us what is going on. We're always here to help you, just like you're always there for us. Okay?"

She smiled at Peter and then glanced at Mary Jane who nodded that she should go on.

"Well," Aunt May said, "I don't know if you know or not, but your Uncle Ben got our home's mortgage through City Mortgage, that big old building down off Broadway."

Both Peter and Mary Jane nodded and waited for her to continue.

"Up until three months ago I made the house payments just fine. And I only have a few years left to go."

"You mean you haven't been able to make them for the last three months?" Peter asked. "Why didn't you say something?" He really wanted to chew her out for not coming to him earlier, but held his opinion to himself. It wouldn't help at the moment from how upset Aunt May looked.

"I didn't want to bother you two," she said. "You were both so busy and all. Besides, I thought I could handle it myself. But now the mortgage company is going to foreclose today unless I catch up on the payments."

"Today?" Peter snapped to attention, the coffee in his hands forgotten. That was the house he grew up in. That had been Aunt May's and Uncle Ben's house for as long as Peter had been alive. How could they suddenly take it away? That just wasn't possible.

Aunt May nodded. "Today, I'm afraid."

"How, May?" Mary Jane asked, her voice soft and understanding. "How did it come to this?"

Aunt May shrugged. "One of the main sources of money I have coming is from some government bonds that mature next month. Just that money alone will keep me just fine for years and years to come. I thought I could hold out until then, but—"

"So you don't have any money now?" Peter asked.

"I'm afraid not. The money from your uncle's life insurance policy ran out three months ago and I only have my social security. And that's not enough to live on and make the house payment."

"That's usually not even enough to buy food on," Peter said.

Aunt May and Mary Jane nodded.

"I went to the bank to see if I could get a loan," she said, not looking up at Peter. "But with my age and my lack of savings, they would only do it if I got someone to co-sign with me."

"I'd love to, Aunt May," Peter said quickly, trying to avoid the embarrassment he could see in her face. She was a very independent woman and she hated asking for help. Just like his wife. No wonder they got along so well.

Aunt May glanced up at him. "You would?"

Peter sighed. "Of course I would. And I wish you'd come to me much earlier. Co-signing a loan is the very least I can do for you."

"Aunt May," Mary Jane said, putting her hand on Aunt May's. "You need to understand that Peter and I are never too busy to help you out if you need something. Ever."

"Listen to her," Peter said, smiling at his aunt.

Aunt May nodded, smiling back and looking relieved.

"Okay," Peter said. "It's almost noon. I have a very important appointment. When do you need me back here to go to the bank with you?"

"Is four o'clock all right? If not, we could—"

"Four o'clock is great. I'll be there."

He jumped up and gave Aunt May a hug and then kissed Mary Jane. "Got some photos to take. See you both at four."

He was out the door before either could complain.

Dr. Catrall sat on the 9 train. He wasn't even sure what direction it was going in, and right now he didn't care. The stations went zipping by, each designed differently from the other. He hadn't noticed that before; each station had a distinct look. The Alice in Wonderland designs at 50th Street, the color murals at 86th Street, the semi-high-tech look of 103rd Street.

He tried to figure out what he should do next. The food had helped clear his mind some. Now was the time to take a logical look at his problem and work out a plan. Any plan.

The men in the diner were right. He couldn't go on running forever. Eventually they would find him. If it hadn't been for Spider-Man the first time and a nice diner owner with a shotgun and a convenient train the second, he would have been caught by now.

But what would happen next time? Who would save him then?

"No one, that's who," he said aloud. The person sitting next to him looked up from his copy of the *Daily Bugle,* snorted, then went back to the sports section. To himself, he continued, *So, you idiot. You need to save yourself. Or figure out a way to get rid of the vial safely.* He glanced down at his briefcase. *Just what am I going to do with you?*

His neighbor got off at 116th Street, his copy of the *Daily Bugle* left behind. Catrall picked it up and quickly scanned the article about Carnage. After reading it, he knew the answer to his question.

Chances were, the answer to his problem would cost him his life. But it would also destroy the "trigger."

And at this point, that was all that mattered.

CHAPTER 7

Ten minutes after leaving Mary Jane and Aunt May, Spider-Man swung onto the Brooklyn Bridge and started across, firing webs at a support pillar, then swinging beyond it to fire a web at the next.

Pillar to pillar to pillar. He had crossed the bridge this way hundreds of times.

The sun was still directly overhead and almost felt warm reflecting off the river. Peter hoped the Indian summer would last for a while. Getting across this bridge when it was coated in ice was never a fun proposition. One really bad winter day he'd even changed into his regular clothes and taken a cab, figuring it would be easier and much safer.

Today, even the river smelled fresh. Peter wasn't sure how that could be, but the ocean-like smell seemed to fill the air over the gray water, completely blocking out the normal rotten stench.

Like the path from the *Daily Bugle* offices to his apartment, the motions to swing across this bridge were routine, though never so much as to be boring. He always got a kick out of watching the boats and the water and waving at the passing cars. But moving from one bridge-anchoring support to the next was so engraved in his subconscious, the pattern so set, that once he started across the bridge the routine allowed him time to think about other things.

Many other things.

Today, he first wondered how his Aunt May could even have hesitated in asking him for help, after all she'd done for him over the years. He could help her every day for the rest of her life and not come close to repaying her for everything.

Why hadn't he seen some signs of her having money problems? Was he really that blind? And why was she so afraid to ask him to simply co-sign a loan? He didn't understand that at all and made a mental note to ask Mary Jane about it later. MJ always had a way of explaining these sorts of things in a way that got through his thick skull.

He reached the middle of the bridge.

His thoughts led him to the early years with his aunt and uncle after his parents had died.

He'd been a small boy when his parents passed on and Aunt May and Uncle Ben had never once complained about being stuck with a child. They had given him everything they could, everything a young boy could hope for, including love, a home, and understanding.

They had even encouraged his fascination with science, a field he still hoped to work in if he ever finished grad school.

But then, in high school, there was the day that

had changed everything. Changed his life, his future, his very way of thinking.

On a trip to a simple science demonstration, he had been accidentally bitten by a spider that had passed through a stream of intense radiation.

Peter had figured out later that the irradiated spider's venom had reacted with his unique blood chemistry to give him the abilities and proportional strength of a spider. He didn't know why exactly. And in experiments since that day he hadn't been able to duplicate the results at all. But it had worked on him.

At first he had let the new power go to his head, trying to make a name for himself in show business as "The Spider Man." Peter knew now that the attempt had been a sad and somewhat pathetic attempt at a freak show act.

But then, when coming out of an afternoon show, a cop had chased a crook past him, and Peter hadn't deigned to help.

It had been beneath him.

It hadn't been his business.

It wasn't his responsibility.

He hadn't wanted to get involved.

All the standard excuses of the weak and cowardly. He had given them all and regretted them every day since.

Later that evening, when he returned home, he

was devastated to learn that his Uncle Ben had been killed by a burglar.

Enraged, Peter brought the burglar to justice because now it *was* his business.

It was *his* uncle that lay in the morgue.

It was *his* aunt who grieved over the loss.

It was *his* feelings that had been trampled by some unknown stranger.

Then he discovered the one fact that would change his life and his very attitude and teach him a very costly lesson. His uncle's death had been his fault.

He could have saved Uncle Ben. The crook he'd let escape earlier that day was the same one who killed his uncle.

From that point onward he made helping people his responsibility. It took the life of his uncle to teach him that with great power must come great responsibility. A lesson he would never forget.

Ever.

And today he had a responsibility to Aunt May and he wasn't going to let her down.

He passed the last section of the bridge and worked his way into Brooklyn's industrial area, moving quickly from one warehouse roof to the next.

The old abandoned school, where they were holding Carnage, was near the edge of the industrial section, and as he approached he realized just how much trouble was coming.

He dropped down onto a roof where he could look over the area.

It was like pictures he had seen of the protests of the sixties. The streets around the school were filled with people carrying signs and screaming with anger about a demon like Carnage being brought into the city again. Peter couldn't say that he blamed them much. He wasn't happy about it either.

Television trucks clogged the side streets and media helicopters dotted the sky, filling the air with a dull roar that at times drowned out the shouts of the protesters.

Police and National Guard troops had the school surrounded, forming lines side by side, facing the thousands of people. Peter couldn't tell if they were keeping the crowds out or were there to keep Carnage in. Probably a little of both.

What a mess.

Someone ran up and hit a cop over the head with a sign. Someone else screamed and the crowd surged forward.

Police rushed extra men to the area and dragged two kicking people toward vans parked on the building's front lawn.

Peter sat on the warm tar roof and shuddered as he surveyed the scene. It looked as if Kasady had already won this round today. People were going to get killed here, whether Carnage did the killing or not.

Wherever Carnage went, chaos followed.

CHAPTER 8

Fiorello glanced around the large gymnasium at millions of dollars of equipment and the hundreds of men and guns that ringed the room. In the center of the room Carnage sat, a skinny-looking, red-haired guy enclosed in four walls of electrically-generated fire. He just sat there smiling, sharing a private joke with no one as he watched all the activity around him.

He didn't look at all like the killer Fiorello knew he was.

But Fiorello had seen what Carnage could do. He'd seen an entire family, except for one child, picked at random, killed without reason by this monster. Even though the guy looked human right now, Fiorello was convinced there wasn't a true human emotion in him.

For the second time Fiorello had walked the entire long distance around the room, checking on every one of his people as well as the twenty Guardsmen, and the generators for the walls of fire around Carnage. Everyone, including the scientists, seemed nervous and ready to get started.

Without exception, everyone was ready.

Every machine was ready.

Every weapon was primed and aimed.

If something happened in the middle of that

room, Carnage wouldn't survive, of that Fiorello was sure. He just wished he could convince his twisting stomach of the same thing.

Fiorello approached O'Keefe, the chief scientist. "You almost ready?"

The tall, thin-framed man didn't even bother to look up from the panel he was working on. "Twenty minutes."

Fiorello nodded and started for the third time around the room to check on every detail once more.

If he had to use the flamethrowers he was damn well going to be ready. He just prayed he wouldn't have to use them.

Spider-Man studied the huge crowd in front of the school for ten minutes, then started scouting for a way inside.

If Carnage was in there, he was going to be, too.

From what Spidey could tell, the old three-story brick school hadn't been used in a good eight or ten years and most of the windows on the upper floors were either broken out or boarded up. From the rundown look of the place, Spidey was surprised the building was even still standing. It must have been bought by some private company who had plans for it. The cities did that a lot and then half the time the old schools just sat, going totally to waste until they were finally condemned and torn down.

The crowd was so large around the front of the school that it overflowed down the side streets. Spidey knew without a doubt that he couldn't get in any of the broken windows on the front or sides without being spotted by two hundred people and three news helicopters circling overhead.

But Carnage was in there and Spidey had been the one to put him away last time. If these experiments didn't work, and somehow he got loose, Spider-Man needed to be there to make sure no one else died.

There were already far too many.

He went to the far side of the roof, away from the crowd and the school, and shot a web at the corner of the warehouse across the street. He waited until his spider-sense told him no one was watching before he swung over.

He circled around the old school from four blocks away, going slowly and carefully so no one would know he was even in the area.

Building by building, he moved around until he had worked his way unnoticed to the back of the school.

The building directly behind the school and slightly to the right had been built in the last five years and it used the school's old ball fields for a parking lot. It looked like a research facility of some sort and had very few windows.

The back of the school also had very few windows and all but one on the top floor were boarded up.

Spidey carefully studied the distance between the two buildings. It was too far to hit with a web shot and too much distance to cover in the air without being seen.

He leaned over the edge and studied the ground. With this building's parking lot and the lot behind the school being mostly full, the cars would give him good cover to get close enough to web up the side of the building.

Quickly, he went down the side of the new building and then, hiding behind a dumpster until his spider-sense told him it was clear, sprinted the short distance across the road and down between the cars.

Within a few seconds of running crouched from car to car he was near enough to the school to hit the wall with a web and be up and through the window in a few seconds.

But there was a new problem. Two guards were stationed against the back of the building and would see him easily if he did that climb. He needed a distraction. Something to draw their attention for just a few seconds.

Looking around, he spotted a Garfield doll attached to the window of a nearby open car. That would work. Garfield dolls were always attention grabbers.

He fished into his pocket and found a twenty dollar bill and quietly webbed it to the lower part of the steering wheel of the car with the Garfield doll, out of sight of passersby, but where the driver would see it. That would cover the cost of the doll easily.

Then he took the doll and moved as close as he could behind the cars and toward the guard on the right.

"You ready for a ride?" he quietly asked the smiling Garfield doll as he attached the cat to his web shooter. "Hope so, because you don't have much choice."

When that guard's head was turned and the other was faced the other direction for a moment, Spidey moved. He shot the doll over the guard's head and against the front windshield of a nearby car, about ten feet beyond the guard.

The doll made a smacking sound as it hit and stuck there, held by the webbing, smiling its Garfield smile up at the guard.

"What in the world!" The guard spun around and trained his machine gun on the still shaking doll. "Where did that come from?" He scanned the parking lot and saw nothing, then scanned the building above. After walking once around the car, staring at the Garfield doll, he shouted to the other guard. "John! Look at this!"

The other guard came running, passing where Peter crouched behind the car without noticing him. As both guards stared at the doll as if it had appeared on the car like magic, Spidey's spider-sense told him the coast was clear.

With a quick web shot to the window ledge, and a quick scramble up the wall, he was through the window without being seen.

He found himself in an empty classroom with high ceilings and a real wood floor. The floor was covered with dust, broken glass, and some scraps of wood. A scratched and very old blackboard still hung on one wall, and some kids had spray-painted gang sayings on it and the other walls.

Someone had built a campfire in one corner of the room and from the trash it looked as if the person had lived here for a few months.

He could imagine going to school in a place like this, when the floors were scrubbed and the desks fairly new. It must have been a good place. Too bad it had gotten like this.

Spidey moved silently to the door leading into the old hall. His spider-sense warned him not to go any farther. Guards were stationed at both ends of the hall and another was at the top of the stairs. There was no going out there without being seen.

A dead end.

He stepped back into the room and looked around again. He could try going out the window and up onto the roof, but just the thought of that sent his spider-sense tingling. There must be soldiers up there, too.

At least they were guarding the place well. Wouldn't do them much good if Carnage got loose, but at least they would stop anyone from coming in and helping him get free.

He moved up toward the old blackboard at the end of the room and turned around. It was then that he saw the old screened vent near the high ceiling. The heating system in this old building must have huge ductwork that went to every space, including the gym where they were doing the experiments.

With a few quick steps he was across the floor and up the wall to the duct.

The screen popped off easily and without a sound he started into the dust and cobweb-filled blackness.

This was one of those days when he felt more like a spider than others.

Dr. Catrall was having a much easier time getting into the heavily-guarded old school than Spidey.

He had simply taken a taxi to Brooklyn and arrived at the new building across the street and behind the school just a few minutes before Spidey reached the school's roof. He had worked in the facility a number of times over the last three years.

What they planned to try on Carnage was work he was familiar with. He was gambling that the employees at this facility hadn't heard about his being missing, since that wasn't the type of information the company would want passed around.

And he had been right.

Besides, they would have never expected him to walk right back into the very place he was running from. Only a crazy person would do that.

He got out of the taxi, and acting as normal as he could, walked right up to the security door without problems. In the distance he could hear the crowds around the school and he could see the helicopters hovering overhead, but no one bothered him at all.

His security code got him inside without a glitch. Obviously they hadn't gotten around to removing his code from the computers in this facility. Either that or it had set off a silent alarm, and he'd turn a corner and find himself facing dozens of armed guards.

But he didn't care.

Most of the workers were at the windows facing the old school watching the crowds. The few that did see him nodded hello. He guessed that on a day like this, with work this important being done, it just seemed logical that he would be here.

Some of the scientists who normally worked in the building were across the street, staffing and running the machines in the school. In fact, the school's proximity to the research facility and the fact that Lifestream Technologies owned both, as well as the other buildings in the area, was the reason it was being used to do the experiments on Carnage.

The radiation treatment they were going to try on Carnage had actually been an offshoot of his work a number of years back. A group of scientists had taken it and run with that offshoot and he had always been more than happy to help them whenever his work allowed. He was inwardly glad that at least some part of his work was being used to help save lives. Or at least stop one killer.

If he could find a way to get the vial into the radiation fields that they would generate around Carnage, it would destroy the contents. The *Bugle* article had included a sidebar mentioning the particulars of the treatment, and Catrall recognized the process instantly. That radiation would alter the molecular structure of his trigger and give the world an inert fluid that would harm no one.

He walked quickly to the elevator and took it down to the basement area, which was mostly used for storage of equipment and old records. In constructing the new labs and office buildings, the contractors had discovered an old maintenance tunnel running along sewer lines from the school, under the new building and to the building on the other side, already owned by the corporation.

The designers, figuring that eventually all three buildings would be connected for maintenance, improved the tunnel slightly and paved it. Many of the machines from the research lab had been taken into the school through the tunnel.

Dr. Catrall knew about the old tunnel and figured it would be the least guarded way into the school.

The basement smelled of old chemicals, and three white lab coats hung on hooks near the exercise room. No one was around at all.

He took one coat and put it on, then headed down the tunnel at a fast walk. He'd have to bluff his way in close to Carnage, but he figured he could do that.

He had to. It was a matter of life and death.

CHAPTER 9

The silence in the huge old gym seemed to fill every corner. The faint noise of the crowd outside and the helicopters overhead didn't even dent the extreme tension.

O'Keefe, in charge of attempting to kill the symbiote without hurting Kasady, walked to the center of the gym, his shoes clicking on the wooden surface. Fiorello stood beside the fire-walled cell and watched him approach.

Everyone in the room watched that walk, including Kasady.

It seemed to take forever.

"We're ready," O'Keefe said as he reached Fiorello. His voice was level and carried to every scientist and armed guard in the room.

Fiorello nodded and did one more quick scan of the gym. Everyone and everything seemed to be in place, so he turned back to O'Keefe. "Let's get it done."

O'Keefe turned and looked up at Kasady. "You have anything to say before we start this process?"

Kasady walked right up to the edge of the fire wall and leered at the two men. "Go on, hit me with your best shot!"

O'Keefe shrugged. "Whether you dare me or not will make very little difference in what is about to happen to you." O'Keefe turned and walked away, motioning for his technicians to start the process.

Fiorello snorted and also turned his back on Kasady, and walked to his station where he could watch.

The experiment had begun.

Dr. Catrall, acting as if he belonged, walked right past one blond-headed guard at the end of the tunnel with nothing more than a nod.

It made sense that anyone coming in from the tunnel would have already passed security measures to get into the other building. So the guard hadn't asked for any identification. Besides, Catrall had on a white coat and was carrying a briefcase. He looked like he belonged, and acting like he did just helped the disguise.

The stairs from the basement toward the main floor of the school were wood and seemed almost rotten, even though they had been used a great deal lately. Someone must have tested them and found them strong enough for this event. Even so, Catrall stayed to the cement wall side of the stairs and moved up slowly to the open door at the top.

Beyond the door was a wide, brightly-lit wooden-floored hall, and another open door beyond leading into the large gym. Dust and garbage littered the corners of the hall and graffiti of all types and colors covered the once-white walls.

Catrall could see guards stationed at regular intervals up and down the hall, and about ten just inside the school's front entrance to the left of the gym. Beyond the front doors the roar of the crowd was constant, like the sound of a waterfall.

From the top of the basement stairs, Catrall could see past the guards at the gym door and into the center of the big room where Kasady was held by the fire-walled cell. Two guards blocked the gym door. Both faced inward.

Catrall could see a lot of other guards inside with guns, plus a bunch of people in fearsome green armor. Some of the scientists he knew hovered around their machines. What looked like bullet-proof screens and bunkers were spaced evenly around the room and in front of certain machines.

Kasady's cell fascinated Catrall the most. It was in and around that cell that the radiation would strike to kill the symbiote in Kasady's blood. Somehow, he needed to get the briefcase inside that radiation just long enough to alter the fluid inside the vial. Not more than a few seconds. In fact, if he could just manage to toss the briefcase through the radiation stream and even break the vial against the fire walls, his task would be complete.

He studied the situation and the guards. He could try running at the cell and just throw the briefcase, but from the looks of the guards, he didn't think he would get close enough to make that plan work. He'd be shot dead without a question and then, if he missed with his throw, the government would have what it wanted.

No, it seemed the only way to get in there, at least close enough to that cell safely with the vial, was to continue the bluff somehow.

The lead scientist—*is that O'Keefe?* Catrall wondered; he couldn't remember—was walking away from the cell, giving the signal that the experiment should begin.

Catrall felt panic filling his stomach and chest.

He had to act now.

He had no choice.

Walking quickly, as if he knew exactly what he was doing, he moved across the hall and said, "Excuse me, please?" to the two guards.

They turned around, guns at the ready, and he held up the briefcase. "O'Keefe needs this," he said, hoping to God it was his name.

Without waiting for them to think fast enough to even try to stop him he walked between them and along the sideline toward where O'Keefe was heading, purposefully not looking at the cell and Kasady until he was even with it.

Neither guard called out behind him. Amazing what and where simply acting and looking like you know what you are doing can get you.

So far he had been lucky. Too lucky.

He kept walking, head down.

He didn't expect his luck to last.

In fact, he expected to die in the next few seconds.

Near the ceiling of the gym, hidden behind the screen of an old ventilation duct, Spider-Man watched the interchange between the scientist and the guy who looked like he was in charge of all the vast numbers of militia and Guardsmen surrounding the cell holding Kasady. He could barely hear their words, but it seemed it was getting close to time to fire everything up.

Sure hope this works, he thought. Having just Kasady in a cell with no chance of him ever becoming Carnage again would help Peter sleep much sounder at night. And from the looks of the crowds outside, the rest of the city, too.

Spidey studied as much of the room as he could see from his position near the ceiling. The place was a fortress, with twenty major gun placements and bullet-proof shields across the gym from each. It was set up to form a deadly crossfire in the center of the gym without harming anyone on any side.

Pretty tricky, but it looked like it might work. Spidey nodded at the good planning and then hoped it wouldn't have to be used. If Carnage got outside of that center area, and the shooting continued, a lot of people would be killed.

Kasady moved to the edge of his cell and sneered something at the two men that Spidey couldn't hear. Knowing Kasady, he guessed it wasn't anything nice.

The scientist and the other guy near the cell seemed to shrug off whatever Kasady had said. Both turned and walked away, the scientist signaling to begin.

Spider-Man watched in rapt fascination as blue rays of light shot out in five directions, from five large machines, and converged on Kasady and his cell.

For a moment, nothing seemed to happen.

Then Kasady screamed and dropped to his knees.

Spidey could see a small trickle of what looked to be blood from the corner of Kasady's nose. But that pseudoblood soon flowed out and around Kasady, covering him with the red-and-black symbiote, forming Carnage.

Carnage stood, the skin flowing and oozing, his mouth open and saliva dripping off the razor teeth.

The blue rays bombarded the cell as Carnage stood against them, his mouth open, a look of intense hatred in his eyes.

Then Spidey's spider-sense went off loud and clear.

Quickly, he forced his gaze away from the scene of Carnage standing against the rays and scanned the room. It didn't take him long to spot the problem. Dr. Catrall, dressed in a white lab coat that made him look like the other scientists, and carrying the black briefcase Spidey remembered from the night before, was striding along near the wall of the gym.

The guards were letting him pass.

Either he belongs here, Spidey thought, *or the guy is totally nuts.*

Quickly, Spider-Man used both hands to pull the grate out of the mouth of the ventilation duct and inward. It made very little noise and he now had an opening if it was needed.

And the way his spider-sense was tingling, it was going to be needed real soon.

Fiorello had made it his job to know, or at least be able to recognize on sight, every scientist working on this project from moment one. And he personally had checked out each and every one of them right down to where they were born, who they had married, and where their spouses and children were this morning.

For the first few seconds after O'Keefe and his people hit Kasady with the rays of visible radiation, Fiorello was struck motionless by the scene, his gaze riveted to the cell.

Kasady changed into Carnage and then Carnage stood against the onslaught. An amazing sight.

But then Fiorello pulled his gaze and attention off the scene in the middle of the room and scanned for problems around the gym.

And it took him a moment to realize what he was seeing.

A problem. A very big problem.

While every guard in the room stood staring at Carnage, a man in a white lab coat was walking along the wall, getting closer and closer to the cell. In his hand he carried a black briefcase with god-knew-what inside. Neither the man nor the brief-case had been cleared by Fiorello.

As Fiorello was about to shout out for the man to stop, the guy glanced around, then turned and started straight for the cell being bathed in blue light and radiation.

"Condition red!" he shouted and his voice shook the room. "Take cover!"

Every weapon in the room raised instantly on his command as every well-trained guard ducked behind bullet-proof shields and took aim. Fiorello pulled out his pistol and aimed it at the unknown man in the white coat. Five more steps and every gun in the room would cut the guy to pieces.

"Stop or die!" Fiorello shouted to the man.

But the guy continued forward.

And then he did the unthinkable. He raised his arm to throw the briefcase at Carnage.

The shout "Condition red!" echoed through the room as Spidey moved.

He was out of the ventilation duct and halfway down the wall when the next shout hit his ears.

"Take cover!"

Around him, shoulders ducked in behind shields and guards readied their weapons, all aimed at the middle of the room. In a few seconds the old gym would be a deadly zone of fiery crossfire, with the shields and positions protecting the guards.

No one could survive for even a half second in the middle of that room and Spidey doubted if even his spider-sense and fast reactions could avoid that many bursts of flame at once. He certainly didn't want to test it.

Spider-Man hit the floor behind a large machine that hummed, but seemed to do nothing else. He jumped up on top of it just as the head of security yelled at Dr. Catrall, "Stop or die!"

Catrall raised his arm to throw the briefcase at Carnage's fire-walled cell.

Spider-Man took aim with both web shooters and hit Dr. Catrall solidly in the back.

The head of security shouted, "Fire!"

Spidey yanked hard, pulling Dr. Catrall off his feet, and sent him and his briefcase sliding across the gym floor just as the room exploded.

Inside the cell, Carnage was a blur of motion as he avoided the deadly fire with lightning-fast reflexes.

Spidey dove behind the nearest machine as the room erupted in a rain of fire mixed in with bullets and even lasers.

"Cease fire!"

The shooting stopped. But the sound continued to echo and echo around and around the room. Wood dropped off the walls and dust filtered down through the air.

Dr. Catrall had come to a stop to the left of a shield and seemed unhurt, his briefcase beside his head still tightly grasped in one hand.

And in the center of the room Carnage still stood, defiant, laughing with joy from all the chaos he saw around him.

Spidey's spider-sense was going wild. Both of the generators had taken numerous shots and were not functioning.

The base of Carnage's cell was also heavily damaged. "I'll bet the old military brains behind this plan didn't think of that option," Spidey said.

As Spidey and the rest of the room watched in horror, the fire walls of Carnage's cell flickered and went out.

Carnage was free.

He stood there laughing, stretching as if he had just woken up from a long nap.

Spider-Man thought quickly. If security released another massive firestorm, they might get lucky and bring down Carnage, but chances were it wouldn't work. But it would kill Dr. Catrall, who still lay in the open against a bullet shield, and it might kill others.

"Don't fire!" Spidey shouted. With a huge leap he jumped into the middle of the room and landed right in front of Carnage. "This guy is all mine!"

Carnage, standing slightly above the floor in the remains of his cell, looked down at Spider-Man and laughed.

CHAPTER 10

Fiorello slowly stood up behind the bullet-proof screen and stared open-mouthed at the destruction. Somehow, the guy with the briefcase had been yanked to safety at the last second by two almost invisible cords.

The crossfire in the center of the room had been as intense as he had hoped, only it hadn't worked. Instead of killing Carnage, he had survived.

And the weapons had destroyed the generators that kept the fire walls in place. The backup in the base of the cell was a charred husk.

As he watched, his worst nightmare occurred.

The fire wall sputtered and shut down completely, leaving Carnage standing in the center.

Unhurt.

Laughing.

And very much free.

"Don't fire!" a shout rang out.

"What—"

Seemingly out of nowhere, Spider-Man dropped in front of Carnage. "This guy is mine!" Spider-Man said.

Fiorello felt a sudden wave of relief inside. Spider-Man was here, and he had put Carnage away last time. He had no idea how the web-slinger had gotten in, but at the moment he was very glad he had.

But Fiorello still had to be ready to do his job.

"Hold your fire!" he shouted at his people. "But be ready for my command!"

He glanced around the gym as Carnage laughed at Spider-Man.

Everyone was ready. All guns reloaded and aimed.

Fiorello just hoped Spider-Man had enough sense to keep Carnage in the middle of the room. Otherwise a lot of people might die.

"Has anyone ever told you," Spider-Man said as he looked up into the laughing mouth and razor-teeth of Carnage, "that you really need to see a dentist? That breath of yours would knock a train off its tracks."

Carnage stopped laughing and stared down at Spider-Man. The red and black of Carnage's symbiote flowed and dripped and swirled over Kasady's body, portraying Kasady's feelings like old colored music lamps attached to a stereo.

Spidey could tell his comment had gotten to Carnage because some of the costume moved faster, turning blacker. The tentacles of costume that sprang off and then retracted did so quicker and with more intensity. Whether that was a good or bad thing would soon be seen.

"It's good to see you joking, Spider-Man," Carnage said, his voice a low, mean growl, "seconds before you die."

"Trust me," Spidey said, "your breath is no joking matter. And speaking of body odor, you really could use—"

Arrows formed on Carnage's right arm and exploded toward Spider-Man from Carnage's fingers like bullets from a gun.

Spidey simply dropped to the floor and instantly sprang back up as the arrows went by and smashed harmlessly into a bullet-proof shield behind him, startling the man and woman stationed there.

"Boy, that's an old trick," Spider-Man said. "Come on. Has prison food made you soft? Or are you just as stupid as you look? I personally would vote for the latter, but of course, I've known you for some time now and—"

"You talk too much," Carnage said.

The moving tentacles of Carnage's costume snaked out like a million strings and formed together into a huge hammer aimed at Spidey's head.

Spidey ducked, but his spider-sense buzzed a warning.

The tentacles dripping from the hammer as it

whizzed by, grabbed him, and yanked him hard toward the cell floor and Carnage.

Spidey pushed off the cell's side with both feet, increasing his speed at Carnage.

In midair, at the last instant, he tucked into a ball and hit the red and black costume square in the chest with his feet.

The impact against Carnage knocked them both off the cell platform and onto the gym floor. They tumbled head-over-heels, Spidey tangled in the flowing, sticky tentacles of the symbiote as it tried to hold him and pull him into a death grip.

Spidey managed to get a hand free and covered Carnage's face with webbing, a trick that hadn't worked in battles before, but this time he was much closer.

At the same time as he webbed Carnage's eyes, he kicked Carnage in the stomach as hard as he could.

A "woof" of air blew out of Carnage's mouth at the impact.

The two twisted and rolled away from each other, both coming to their feet on separate sides of the cell like two boxers in a ring.

They both stepped slowly back up onto the cell platform.

"I'm going to tear your arms off and eat them, Spider-Man," Carnage said.

"I'd offer you a good Chianti to go along with

the meal," Spider-Man said, "but Muscatel is more your speed."

Carnage picked up the chair and threw it at Spider-Man.

But this time Spidey's spider-sense warned him that tentacles of the symbiote costume rode with the chair like they had with the hammer a moment before.

Spidey ducked, while at the same time hitting Carnage with webs around his feet.

As the chair sailed past and the tentacles reached for him, Spidey yanked on the webs, which snapped Carnage onto his back. A loud smacking sound forced the tentacles up and away.

"Now it's time to do something about that breath!" Spider-Man said.

With a quick leap, he was on Carnage in a flash, his fists pounding into Carnage's head like the rapid pounding of pistons in a high-speed engine.

His fists were a blur.

He imagined the faces of all those dead people floating up in front of his eyes and for each one he got angrier and angrier.

For each dead face he hit Carnage.

He pounded that ugly face again and again and again.

The force of the blows was so hard that Carnage's head smashed through the floor and into the machinery below.

Before Spider-Man could knock him out completely, a hammer-like fist formed in the middle of Carnage's suit. It caught Spidey square in the stomach before his spider-sense could warn him.

The fist launched him into the air like a rocket and toward the equipment where Dr. Catrall still lay.

He twisted while still in the air and saw Carnage stagger to his feet. That guy had one tough head.

But before Spidey could land and spring back to the battle, or even catch his breath, he heard the words he hoped he would never hear again.

"Open fire!"

His spider-sense went wild.

Catrall was in trouble.

Big trouble.

He wouldn't live through another barrage of fire like the last one.

Spidey hit the floor like a tight spring and bounded instantly to Dr. Catrall. He grabbed the doctor and yanked him behind a shield as flames and artillery flew everywhere.

"Are you all right?"

Dr. Catrall blinked a few times and then clutched the briefcase to his side and nodded.

"Yeah, I think so," he said, just barely loud enough for Spider-Man to hear.

"Stay here," Spider-Man shouted over the din.

Catrall nodded and Spidey turned his attention back to the middle of the room just as a huge explosion sent smoke and wood and dust everywhere.

"Cease fire!"

In two quick leaps Spidey was beside the guy giving the orders, staring into the dust. "Did you get him?"

The guy glanced for just a second at Spider-Man from under his Mets cap and then said, "I sure hope so."

"If not," Spidey said, "let me have another go at it. I almost had him."

The guy nodded and then as the dust slowly settled and silence fell over the room, Spider-Man saw what he feared most.

Nothing.

The center of the room was empty except for the remains of the cell.

Carnage was gone.

"Oh, no!" the guy in charge said softly beside Spider-Man.

"You got that right."

Spidey could feel the knot in his stomach tightening as he saw, near the front door, two guards tossed aside like kindling, their broken bodies left in piles, their weapons snapped in half. Carnage had gone that direction during the covering explosion and before Spidey took off after him, he needed to find out from Dr. Catrall just what was going on.

He turned and then stopped.

Dr. Catrall was also gone.

CHAPTER II

The warm afternoon sun made the light lunch at the Parker apartment very pleasant.

Mary Jane had fixed herself and Aunt May some grilled tuna sandwiches and a small shrimp salad. They were enjoying each other's company now that the problem with the house payments was almost solved.

The Feed 'Em All program sponsored by the *Daily Bugle* was showing on the television that Mary Jane had turned on in the living room.

"You know," Aunt May said, touching her mouth with her napkin and indicating the newscast, "that seems like such a good thing for the newspaper to do. Peter should be very proud to work there."

Mary Jane laughed lightly. "I'm sure he is. I suppose the program is a good one, but it seems to be more of a publicity stunt than anything else."

Aunt May glanced at Mary Jane with a puzzled look. "I'm not sure how that could be."

"If they really wanted to do some good," Mary Jane went on, "they'd fund more money for the regular shelters and programs to help the homeless find jobs, and to care for the children. What they're planning on doing today is just drawing attention to the problem without really finding any long-term solutions."

Aunt May nodded. "I suppose you're right. But at least their intention is in the right place. As my late husband used to say, 'intention is fifty percent of anything.' "

Mary Jane was about to answer when the television switched to bright red words: *Special News Bulletin.*

An announcer came on holding a microphone. He looked very upset. A large crowd could be seen behind him surrounding an abandoned-looking school house. Ambulances and police cars with lights flashing seemed to be parked everywhere.

The announcer nodded at someone off-camera, then looked straight into the camera and said, "This afternoon, at the old Brooklyn High School, the notorious serial killer, Carnage, escaped police custody."

Mary Jane thought she was going to be sick. The sandwich she had just finished suddenly felt more like a brick in her stomach.

"For a short time," the announcer went on, "Spider-Man was able to hold Carnage inside the school gym after an as-yet unidentified man, posing as a scientist, barged in and caused Carnage's release from his high-tech cell. At two separate times during the event, gunfire was heard inside the building. We have no information at the moment as to how this man got into the building and freed Carnage or why he would want to do so."

"Oh, no," Mary Jane said.

"Is the news upsetting you, dear?" Aunt May asked.

Mary Jane didn't take her gaze from the screen.

"We have further information that in a hail of gunfire and explosions, Spider-Man—"

Aunt May clicked off the television and turned back to the table. "Now, isn't that much better?"

Mary Jane wanted to scream and run to the set, push Aunt May out of the way and turn it back on to find out what had happened to Peter. Instead, she took a deep breath and somehow managed to stay calm enough that Aunt May didn't seem to notice.

"That's so much nicer," Aunt May said. "I never listen to the news at my house. There's just so much violence, and since Peter's uncle died I just can't stand it." She took a bite of her sandwich and went on. "And that awful vigilante, that Spider-person. I wish they'd just deport him or something."

Aunt May brushed the crumbs off the table and into her hand, then sprinkled them on her plate while Mary Jane fought to retain her composure.

"Here," Mary Jane said, standing. "Let me drop those in the sink and get us some more coffee."

"That would be wonderful," Aunt May said.

Mary Jane took both plates, doing her best to keep her hands from shaking, and headed for the kitchen.

She quickly dumped the dishes in the sink and turned on the small television on the counter, keeping the sound low enough so that Aunt May wouldn't hear.

She leaned in close to the set, desperate for any information at all as the cameras panned from a helicopter over the school, replaying the battle that had gone on inside.

"Let me repeat," the announcer said over the pictures of the old school. "No one was killed. Four have minor injuries. Spider-Man was able to contain Carnage for a short time inside the school. But then, in an unexpected explosion, the feared serial killer managed to escape."

Mary Jane leaned her head against the set, fighting to hold back the tears as the announcer was handed a piece of paper. After perusing it, he went on.

"We have learned that the man responsible for freeing Carnage is Lifestream Technologies employee, Dr. Eric Catrall." The screen changed to a still picture of the doctor smiling at the camera. "Dr. Catrall also disappeared from the scene without a trace."

The announcer's face replaced the pictures of smoke pouring out through the boarded-up windows of the old school. "Spider-Man was seen swinging away after the battle. We do not know if he was tracking Carnage. Police have notified the Fantastic Four, the Avengers, and other agencies in the surrounding areas to be on the lookout. We will have further news as it develops."

Mary Jane shut off the set and stood up straight, taking deep breaths. "Please be all right, Peter," she said softly. "Please."

She took a few more deep breaths, then poured her and Aunt May each a cup of coffee and went back into the dining room.

She had just set the cups on the table and started to take her seat when the front door opened and Peter walked in.

Spider-Man couldn't understand how someone as well known as Carnage could get out of the building without anyone seeing which direction he had gone. But somehow, either as Carnage or as Kasady, he had managed it, along with Dr. Catrall.

He had done a quick search of the surrounding area, then swung by the *Daily Bugle* with pictures of the fight and the escape. Before dropping down into the gym he'd set up his camera on automatic in the ventilation shaft. He hoped he'd gotten some good shots. He and MJ could use the money.

Now, he was late getting back to the apartment to meet Aunt May. Not even Carnage escaping could cause him to miss helping his aunt. He owed her far too much.

He'd changed into Spider-Man outside the *Daily Bugle,* then made it to the apartment in record time.

He had again changed in the alley below his apartment, this time back to regular clothes, and then had run up the stairs.

When he opened the door Mary Jane was standing at the dining table near his Aunt May. Aunt May smiled at him, but MJ gave out a little shriek and ran to him, grabbing him by the neck before he could even get the door closed, and hugged harder than she had in a long time.

"You heard, huh?" he whispered into her thick mane of hair.

She nodded. "I was so worried."

"It's so nice," Aunt May said, a slight blush filling her cheeks, "to see you two lovebirds so lovey-dovey."

"Having my husband almost killed by a psycho," Mary Jane whispered to Peter, "always brings out the romance in me."

"Oh, I like that," Peter whispered and gave her a hug.

"Well," Aunt May said, standing and brushing off her dress. "I need to stop at home and get some papers before going to the bank. Now Peter, are you sure you—"

Peter held up his hand for her to stop. "Aunt May, of course I want to sign the note. I will meet you at the bank."

Aunt May smiled, obviously very happy. She picked up her large purse and hustled toward the front door, giving the two young people, still holding on to each other, a wide berth.

Peter unwrapped himself from Mary Jane just in time to step over and give his aunt a quick hug.

"Now don't be late," she said as she opened the door. "The bank closes at six o'clock sharp."

"I'll be there at five," Peter said.

Aunt May smiled. "That would be perfect. Thank you."

She closed the door and the next thing Peter knew Mary Jane was giving him a very hard and very passionate kiss.

After the long kiss he spent the next few minutes giving her exact details of what had occurred at the school and then he headed for the shower.

Fifteen minutes later he returned to the living room, dressed and ready to go help his aunt.

Mary Jane was standing at the open window, looking over the nearest buildings and the city street below. She looked sad and she was twisting her wedding ring.

Peter moved behind her and gave her a hug, putting his head on her left shoulder. "Something bothering you beside my fight with Carnage?"

Mary Jane sort of shrugged and then, without turning around, said, "Yeah, sort of."

"You want me to guess?" Peter said, softly, nuzzling her hair and neck gently.

She laughed lightly, but Peter could tell her heart wasn't in it.

"It's just that I wish I could do more," she blurted out after a moment.

Peter stepped back enough for her to turn and face him. Then, with his right hand he stroked her arm in support, telling her silently that she should go on.

She looked like she was about to cry, but was holding it back. "It's just that you're helping Aunt May keep her house. And you help total strangers every day by risking your life as Spider-Man. But I can't even help pay the rent."

Peter smiled and kissed her. He felt very relieved that was all it was. For a moment he had been concerned that she was sick, or that something else was going on.

He took a deep breath and let it out slowly. "It's the fact that you want to help that matters. You know that."

She nodded, not convinced at all. "Aunt May said that your uncle always said that."

"He did," Peter said. "And it's true. Look, I know for a fact that you put more money into our household than I did for a long time. So now it's my turn. You'll be back working soon and then you'll be making a lot more money than I do. When that happens are you going to hog it all and not share any with me?"

"Of course not," she said, smiling at him.

"So let me share a little while I make the big bucks."

She laughed and her laugh made him smile. He loved it when she laughed.

"Big bucks?" she asked. "Yeah, right."

"Stabbed through the ego." He pretended to stagger back while holding his chest.

She laughed and hugged him.

"Feeling better?"

"Not really," she said, smiling at him. "But thanks."

"I guess I'm just having one of those days," he said. "First Carnage gets away and now this."

They both laughed.

Mary Jane looked at Peter. "Maybe we got time for a repeat performance from this morning? That would definitely make me feel better."

"Well—"

The phone rang on the table behind them.

"Hold that thought," he said and grabbed it.

"Peter," Kate Cushing, the city editor of the

Daily Bugle said without so much as a hello. "I need you and your camera to get to the Twentieth Precinct station over on 82nd and Columbus."

"What's happening?" Peter asked, glancing at the worried look that suddenly crossed Mary Jane's face.

"You know the mad scientist who screwed everything up in Brooklyn?"

"Yeah," Peter said. "I'm afraid I do. A Dr. Catrall."

"That's the one," Kate said. "They have him in custody."

"On my way," Peter said.

He hung up and turned to Mary Jane. "They have Dr. Catrall in jail and I need to get down there. You wanted to do something to help."

Mary Jane nodded.

"Meet Aunt May for me at the bank and tell her I will be there. I just might be a few minutes late. Tell her not to worry."

"I'll take care of it," she said.

Peter kissed her hard. "Thanks."

He sprinted for the bedroom, pulling off his clothes and exposing his Spider-Man suit as he ran. He webbed up his clothes in a backpack-like bundle on his back before putting on his mask and gloves.

Seconds later he was out the window and headed across town.

CHAPTER 12

The isolation cell of the Twentieth Precinct smelled of urine and wet cardboard and was ten degrees too warm on this fall afternoon. In the winter, prisoners complained of being too cold, and in the summer they sweated continuously.

An open, stained toilet sat against one wall with a sink above it to the left. A roll of toilet paper was stuck on the cold water tap and the faucet dripped continuously into a rusted drain.

Along the right wall was a cot with a thin brown-stained mattress over hard plywood. There were no sheets. The cell had been painted a light brown and was scratched above the sink and cot, evidence of many former occupants.

The door to the cell was the same color as the walls, with only a small, barred window in it. A barred window, open to the elements except for a screen, looked out on a blank brick wall. Very little light ever filtered down past that building and through the window. The sounds of the city barely drifted in, even during the noisiest times.

Dr. Eric Catrall sat on the bunk, his head in his hands, his gaze glassy as he stared at the floor and into the horror his life had become in the last few days.

Outside, upside down on the wall over the window, Spider-Man snapped a few quick shots of Dr. Catrall sitting on the bunk, then tucked the camera into the pocket of his costume.

"Excuse me, Doctor," Spidey said.

It took a moment, but then Dr. Catrall sat up straight and looked slowly toward the door.

"Wrong way," Spidey said. "Check the window."

Dr. Catrall looked in Spider-Man's direction, shock covering his face. "You! You've come to get me out?"

Spidey laughed. "Not hardly." He tugged on the wire screen and bars, pretending they were too strong for him, even though he could have bent them like George Reeves used to do in the early days of television. "You're stuck, I'm afraid."

"Well then," Catrall said, turning away from the window, his voice tired. "What do you want?"

"Well, for starters, since we're sort of in this together, you might want to tell me just what's going on. Why did you want to free Carnage?"

Dr. Catrall looked shocked. He stood quickly and moved to the window. "You don't understand. I never intended to free Carnage. Ever. You've got to believe me on that."

"All right," Spidey said. "Say for kicks and giggles that I believe you. What exactly *were* you doing in that old school this afternoon? Sightseeing?"

Catrall twisted his head trying to look directly at Spider-Man, who was still hanging upside down outside the window.

"Hang on a second." Spidey dropped around and then held himself so he was right side up looking directly at the Doctor through the window. "Now let's hear it."

Catrall nodded and took a deep breath. "It was the work I was doing."

"With Lifestream?"

Catrall glanced at Spidey through the bars and wire screen. "You know about it?"

"Only that you worked for them and that you were highly respected before all this. How about jumping right to the chase and telling me why the FBI was after you last night?"

Catrall nodded. "My work. They were after me because I invented a liquid that, when touched by humans, turns them into crazed, killing animals."

Spider-Man shook his head. "Why in the world would you invent something like that?"

"It was an accident! A simple by-product on the way to a compound that would do exactly the opposite. You can read about my work anywhere and know that I was striving to find a solution to violence of all types. This *trigger*, as I call it, was just a step along the way."

"So what happened?"

"Lifestream was monitoring my work, ready to

sell it to covert government operations. They were going to put it into the drinking water of entire countries."

"Your trigger? Why?" Spidey was having a hard time comprehending the problem.

Dr. Catrall looked upset. "Don't you see? One tiny speck of the liquid touching the skin will turn a normal human being into a total killer. I stole all of it and had it in that briefcase. An entire vial. Enough to turn every man, woman, or child in this country into violent killers."

Spider-Man hung outside the window and tried to let what he had just heard sink in. He didn't like the possible outcomes.

"A few more questions, Doctor?"

Dr. Catrall nodded.

"If Lifestream was monitoring your work, why bother to steal the vial and run? Wouldn't they just be able to reproduce your work from the records?"

For the first time Catrall smiled. "At Lifestream it was normal for everyone to put their files in codes. I'm sure they think that given enough time they can decipher my codes, but they won't." Catrall laughed.

"And why won't they?"

"Because I didn't use a code." Again Catrall laughed, his voice going higher and higher.

It was clear to Spider-Man that this guy had been driven almost insane and was moving farther and farther in that direction very quickly.

"No code?"

Catrall nodded. "No code. Everything I wrote down or put in their computers was total gobbledygook. I have a photographic memory, so I just trusted my own mind. Now I'm very, very glad I did."

"So the sample you were carrying was the only way the government could duplicate your work, right? Except for making you tell them."

Catrall nodded, the smile disappearing from his face. "But if that vial breaks, all is lost. The stuff won't break down for years. If the rains wash it into the ground water, the entire city might go crazy. The only thing that can neutralize it is certain types of radiation. The same radiation they were using on Carnage."

Spider-Man was starting to get the picture. "So you wanted to toss the vial of stuff into the radiation bombarding Carnage so that the only sample would be harmless? And if the radiation had hit it, then no one would be able to copy it. Right?"

Catrall nodded. "I never meant to set that monster free. You have to believe me."

"Actually, I think I do," Spidey said. "So, do the police have the vial now, or did you stash it somewhere?"

Catrall suddenly started sobbing.

"Yo, Doc. Talk to me. Don't check out on me now."

Catrall glanced up at the window, tears flowing down his face. "He tortured me until I told him. I couldn't stop myself. I hate pain and—"

Catrall totally lost control, huge racking sobs breaking through the room and echoing off the walls behind Spider-Man.

"Carnage has the vial?" Spidey asked, more afraid than he had been in years. "You're telling me a psycho now has the ability to turn the entire nation into psychos like himself?"

All Catrall did was sob uncontrollably, muttering over and over that he had failed and why couldn't he just have died.

Spidey moved away from the window as a guard came in to check on Catrall. He doubted there was much anyone could do for the doctor now. The guilt in his mind was driving him crazy.

Spider-Man had a clear understanding of that problem.

He hit the opposite building with a web and swung over, then climbed quickly to the roof, wondering why Carnage didn't kill Catrall when he was done. He wouldn't get an answer out of Catrall now, if Catrall even knew. Then again, Carnage had been known to not kill someone you'd expect him to kill; more of that chaos-worship of his.

When he arrived on the roof, he gazed in two directions over about twenty blocks of the busy city.

Such a huge city. Where am I going to look?

One crazed man who loved doing the unexpected. How could he be found in a city this size?

Spider-Man sat down on the roof ledge and stared out over the buildings and the busy streets, trying to calm down and just think.

Carnage was out there with a vial of fluid that would wreak chaos over the city and maybe the country if he could find a way to spread it.

So where was he?

And how was Spider-Man going to find him in time?

CHAPTER 13

CARNAGE IN NEW YORK

The soft music from the Yanni CD playing in the background could barely be heard over the talking of the twenty-five party guests. They mingled in the deep-carpeted penthouse living room and spilled out onto the balcony that overlooked Central Park. The warm sun gave the room a party feel and the guests were sipping freely from drinks kept constantly refreshed by two waiters.

David Ballard glanced around the lavishly furnished room, noting that he knew most everyone here from other parties. It seemed that even a city the size of New York had a very small party circuit at certain social levels.

This room had obviously been decorated simply to impress guests. It had a cold, sterile feel even though the carpet was a light tan with deep pile and the walls were off-white. The furniture seemed stark and uncomfortable-looking and no one was sitting. Huge decorative vases sat on all the end tables like signs saying *Don't Bump Me, I Break*. Ugly metal statues filled nooks, and garish oil paintings were spotted on the walls under perfect spot lighting. This was some designer's idea of a perfect living room that made the word "living" laughable.

David held the cold glass of tonic in his hand

and looked around. There was no place in the entire room to safely put down a drink. The people out on the balcony were placing theirs on the railing where a slight nudge would send the drinks thirty stories down onto the heads of people on the sidewalk. Not a good idea, but at least better than what he had available.

He took another sip and resigned himself to a cold wet hand until a passing waiter came by.

He let his gaze wander out over the city and then back to the tall, brown-haired, green-eyed young woman in a leather coat standing near the door. She was the reason he was here.

He was a Wall Street broker and close friends with the owners of this penthouse, Bob and Cindy Higgens. They'd invited him to join them for an afternoon of fun, as they called it. He couldn't imagine how a cocktail party could ever be fun. But Cindy had said it was for the good cause of "Feed 'Em All," the program sponsored by the *Daily Bugle*. On her instructions, he'd put together a large sack of old sweaters and coats and had added it to the pile forming in the middle of the living room.

The plan was that at six they would all go downstairs and across the street to the park where the "Feed 'Em All" program was set up to start, hauling their donations, along with their checkbooks, to the bigger party. There, they'd all get their pictures taken for the newspaper and their jobs would be done.

Doing his good deed for the day was all well and good, as far as he was concerned, but David would rather have just donated to a local shelter and been done with it. But the reason he had accepted the invitation was that Cindy Higgens had told him her friend Nancy would be there also.

Nancy had been an infatuation of his for months. She was a tall actress who had worked a few off-Broadway shows. She had family wealth and a sense of humor that matched his. Her green eyes somehow drew him into staring at her and she had caught him numbers of times. David was six-foot-two and she was one of the few women he could look squarely in the eye. They'd done the I'm-attracted-to-you dance at a few previous parties and he hoped this would be the one where they could finally get to know each other better.

A lot better.

He'd arrived early and been deadly bored until she'd come in ten minutes ago. She had smiled and waved at him while she did her duty and talked the prescribed amount of time to their hosts. He was headed across the room to rescue her and help her out of her leather coat when a woman behind him near the balcony screamed.

Not the scream of dropping a drink or being caught by a joke, but the scream of pure terror.

He spun around just in time to see a red monster drop down onto the balcony from the roof of the penthouse.

A monster from any child's nightmares, with razor teeth, bug eyes, and a red and black skin that seemed to be in constant motion, dripping and flowing and reforming around that hideous being.

"Carnage," someone whispered to his right.

David's blood chilled. He knew that name and he'd read about the psycho-killer. He'd just never expected to get this close to the guy.

David backed slowly toward the main door where Nancy stood frozen beside the owners of the apartment. Maybe with some luck they could make a break for it.

"It seems we're having a party here," Carnage said, smirking at the frozen and terrified guests. "How come I wasn't invited?"

No one answered, but like David most of them slowly backed away from the creature.

To David's right, out of the corner of his eye, he saw Bob Higgens slowly reach into a drawer near the door and pull out a small revolver.

Like a movie in slow motion, Bob raised the gun to fire at Carnage, but before he could a pointed lance formed on Carnage's arm and shot down his arm and across the room.

It spiked through Bob's arm, pinning him to

the wall with a thud and a spray of blood.

"Now that wasn't a very nice invitation," Carnage said.

Everyone moved at once.

Screaming.

Shouting.

Fighting to save themselves.

Carnage had won again.

Chaos ruled.

David jumped backwards, grabbing Nancy, who seemed frozen in terror. He desperately pulled her toward the front door.

Nancy doubled over and threw up, the retching noise lost in the screams.

In the center of the chaos, Carnage stood.

Ten arrows formed from his fingers and shot out, pinning a waiter to a wall as he tried to make a break for the kitchen.

A long tendril of skin yanked another man off the ledge outside the patio as he tried to crawl away along the outside of the building. The tendril picked the man up, turned him upside down, and like a child, used the man's head as a hammer to pound a patio table into oblivion.

An artist type, with a beard and long coat, picked up a metal statue of a nude woman with her arms stretched over her head. When Carnage's back was turned for an instant he threw it hard at the back of the massive black and red head.

A tendril formed on the back of Carnage's head and caught the statue like a professional baseball player would catch an underhand throw from a child.

Carnage turned around, saliva dripping from his razor teeth. "So you like playing catch, huh?" he said to the man.

The statue shot at the man so fast the guy didn't even have time to put up his hands.

The statue of the woman went through the artist's stomach and out his back, before smashing into two huddled guests near the couch.

David froze, holding Nancy as she gasped for air, her eyes locked on the dead eyes of her friend, Cindy. David hadn't even seen Carnage kill her, but there she lay, dead in front of them.

After a moment everyone in the room stopped and Carnage surveyed his party. Only the sounds of gasping and crying filled the room. The stereo had been smashed, letting in the street sounds from the city and the park beyond.

"So," Carnage said, stepping over the body of the artist and moving to the pile of old clothes in the center of the carpet. "Would someone like to tell me what the occasion of this joyful party might be?"

He scanned the room, but no one answered.

David didn't take his eyes off the tooth-filled mouth of the creature. In his arms Nancy sobbed lightly, no longer aware that she and everyone around her was about to die.

"Cat got everyone's tongues?" Carnage said when no one answered him. "Here, let me see?"

A half dozen tendrils of black and red ooze shot off his body and grabbed a woman around the chest and head. The woman, who David remembered was named Claudia, had on a formal, long black dress and had been standing against the edge of the patio door behind Carnage. After a moment, that dress was showered in blood.

David wanted to be sick, wanted to throw up everything he had ever eaten, but somehow he kept his gaze on Carnage.

Slowly Carnage turned and looked around the room. "Now, would someone tell me the occasion of this party?"

"It was a benefit," David heard himself saying and Carnage turned his gaze directly at him. The huge bug eyes focused at him chilled David to the bone, but it was clear now that they were all going to die. At this point, anything might work to give them extra time, including answering the monster.

"Go on," Carnage said.

David took a deep breath. "For the homeless. They, the *Daily Bugle*, and others, trying to feed the homeless all one meal across in the park there." David pointed out over the balcony, past the five people who huddled there. "The clothes were for the homeless. We were planning to go over there, into the park, at six when the meal started."

Carnage bowed slightly at David. "Thank you, good sir," he said with a smile. Then he turned and strode out on the balcony and looked down over the park. As he went David could see a black briefcase wrapped in his costume on his back and protected like it was a part of his body.

Carnage stared down at the park. When he turned back around he was smiling.

He strode back into the center of the room. "It seems," he said, "that I now have a date across the street at six."

He looked around at the twenty or so people still alive, all standing or huddled as far from him as they could get.

"But it would appear," he said, "that I have some time to kill between now and then."

David felt shivers going up and down his back as Carnage looked each of them over very carefully.

In his arms, Nancy continued to sob quietly, never taking her gaze away from the open eyes of her dead friend.

CHAPTER 14

It was a little after five by the time Spider-Man swung toward the offices of the *Daily Bugle*.

The sky had turned dark; the only trace of the beautiful fall day was a golden streak on the western horizon. The city's lights were on and the chill was quickly returning to the air. The night promised to be colder than the night before, now that the cloud cover had lifted and the rain had stopped.

Spidey had spent the last forty-five minutes paying no attention at all to the fall sunset or the chilling air. His focus had been on one thing and one thing only. Finding Carnage.

He had searched every location in the city where he could think that Carnage might drop the deadly liquid into the water or food supply lines of the city. The water treatment plants, the main pumping stations, even the water towers and containment tanks on the tops of the tallest buildings.

He'd checked them all without luck.

Kasady, or Carnage, was nowhere to be seen.

Spider-Man swung onto the roof of the *Daily Bugle* and quickly changed into his civilian clothes on the way down the three flights of stairs to the newsroom. *Maybe one of the reporters has a lead,* he hoped.

This evening the big room wasn't as noisy as it was that morning, so Peter didn't walk into the wall of sound that he normally did when coming through the main door. But the place still had the excitement of a carnival on Saturday night.

Twenty reporters sat or stood near desks in the giant room, most of them pounding on keyboards in front of computer terminals. Through the conference room's big double doors, Peter could see that all the television monitors were working. Another twenty or so people milled around the center of that room, with Jonah Jameson, the publisher, right in the middle.

"Peter!"

Peter turned away from the conference room to see Glory Grant, Jonah's secretary, waving for him to come into Jonah's office near the other side of the newsroom.

Glory was a no-nonsense type of person who somehow managed to work around Jonah every day, sometimes seven days a week, without going totally, screaming crazy.

Peter had no idea how she managed her job as well as she did, but he was glad it was someone as nice as her. It balanced Jonah's mean streak.

He wound his way through the desks and followed Glory into her cubicle outside Jonah's office. She pointed to the phone, half smiling at him. "Your wife has been waiting." Glory used a folder to fan the phone like she was trying to cool it off. "She sounds upset."

The sudden realization that Peter had totally forgotten his appointment with Aunt May shocked him to his very core.

He glanced up at the wall clock that read five minutes after five. He was late. He had been so concerned with finding Carnage that not once had he thought of Aunt May.

Not once.

Glory laughed. "From the look on your face, you know what you did wrong. I'll leave you alone."

"Thanks," Peter said as she disappeared into Jonah's office and closed the door.

"MJ," Peter said into the phone.

"Oh, thank heavens," he heard MJ say on the other end of the line, the relief very obvious in her voice. "I thought something had happened to you."

"It's a long story."

"Carnage?" Mary Jane said softly.

"Yeah," Peter said. "If I don't find him soon things could get really ugly around the city." He paused for a moment, then decided to tell her the entire truth. "A lot of people are going to die."

Silence greeted Peter on the other end of the line.

Peter glanced up at the clock again. "Look, I

have the five minutes it's going to take to sign the loan. Is Aunt May all right?"

"She seems to be," Mary Jane said. "Just a little worried. But the bankers here are being very nice to both of us, fixing us coffee and everything. In fact, it's very surprising how nice they're all being."

"Good. I'll see you in a few minutes. I'll swing right over."

"Peter—"

"Yes," Peter said.

"Be careful."

"I will. See you in a few minutes."

He hung up the phone. How could he have forgotten? How?

He wanted to scream at himself, kick himself around the block and then back again.

Aunt May was everything to him and now that he had a chance to help her, he forgot.

He just forgot!

What kind of nephew was he?

What was wrong with him?

"Everyone well, I hope?" Glory said as she came back out of Jonah's office.

"For the moment," Peter said. "But if I don't get my body outta here real quick-like I may be dead. And I will deserve to be, without a doubt."

Glory laughed. "I understand that. Good luck."

"Thanks," Peter said.

Still in shock at his forgetting, he headed out through the big newsroom, working his way in and out of the desks, aiming for the main doors. He'd go back up the stairs and off the roof like he'd come in. Five minutes in the bank would be all it would take. Just five minutes and then he could go back to searching for Carnage.

"Parker!"

Again his name rang out through the big room, only this time he knew who it was without looking. Jonah.

He turned away from the main entrance and headed toward where Jonah stood near the big conference room door.

Jonah was dressed up a little more than normal. His striped shirt almost looked pressed and his top button was actually buttoned. However, his tie was still loose and his normal big, smelly cigar still stuck out of the corner of his mouth like it would drop at any moment.

"Parker, I need you and your camera down at the *event*. I want as many shots of this as I can get."

For a moment Peter thought about objecting, saying he had another appointment, but then thought better of it. Arguing with Jonah was never a good thing to do at the best of times. And right now he and MJ needed the money much more than he needed to take a chance getting fired by Jonah.

Besides, as Spider-Man, he could get to the bank, sign the papers and still get to Central Park before a normal person could get there in a taxi.

"So it's going well?" Peter asked.

Jonah beamed. "Sure is." He waved his arms at the walls of monitors behind him. "Even with that Carnage creep getting loose this morning we're getting great coverage from all the news services all over the world."

"Sir!" One of the young interns working the wireroom ran up holding a piece of paper. "There's something happening across the street from the food service vans. In the penthouse of the corner building."

The kid thrust the police scanner report at Jonah. "I thought you should know."

Jonah glanced at it and turned to one of the technicians. "Scan camera ten off the park and across the street. Get me a closeup of the penthouse on that building on the corner."

Jonah thrust the paper at Peter and turned his attention to the camera.

It was a basic police report. Screams had been heard coming from the penthouse an hour ago and blood had been seen dripping through the ceiling of the apartment below. No police had been able to get up there by either the stairs or elevator. Two cops were already missing. The SWAT team was being called in and setting up.

Peter looked up at the monitors showing the huge food service area and the thousands of people already crowding into the park.

"Oh, no," he said softly.

The monitor showing the picture from camera ten slowly panned over the crowd and focused on the building behind the food service trucks.

Slowly it panned up the wall, floor by floor. Peter knew he could climb that building far faster than that camera was panning, but like everyone in the big conference room now, he stood and waited.

Finally it stopped on the penthouse.

It took a moment for Peter to realize just what he was seeing as the camera slowly zoomed in and then focused.

A man's body was draped over the railing of the penthouse.

Beside the body stood Carnage, staring out over the thousands of people in the park below, drool running off his razor-sharp teeth like a hungry person seeing food for the very first time.

Jonah swore a blue streak as pandemonium broke loose in the room.

Then Peter visibly shuddered. His worst nightmare looked as if it was about to come true.

On the balcony rail beside Carnage was a black briefcase.

It was open and empty.

CHAPTER 15

Mary Jane hung up the phone and looked around at the comfortable, but business-like setting of the bank loan offices. The place was comfortably warm and smelled of oak and potting soil. A dark-haired secretary named Randie sat behind a large desk in front of two doors. At the moment she seemed to be very busy typing something into her computer. But earlier she had been very friendly, helping Aunt May get comfortable and getting her a cup of coffee.

Aunt May was still sipping that cup of coffee in the waiting area across from Randie's desk. She was reading a copy of a recent *Reader's Digest* and looked calm and almost relaxed, even though Peter was late. How she managed that while on the verge of losing her house was beyond Mary Jane. Maybe after that many years of being alive and seeing the ups and downs of life, this sort of thing just didn't bother her anymore.

But Mary Jane wasn't that old or that secure. Right now Peter's lateness was driving her nuts. Thank heavens she had found him. He would have never been this late if something really important hadn't come up. She knew her husband very well and she knew how important it was for him to help his aunt.

But Peter felt responsible for that monster, Carnage. And if it came to choosing between saving Aunt May's house and saving someone from being killed by Carnage, she knew Peter would make the right choice.

Mary Jane just hoped he didn't have to make that choice in the next ten minutes.

She glanced at the decorative clock sitting on the secretary's desk. Ten after five. There were only fifty minutes to get a check from the bank and get two blocks to the loan company. They would make it if Peter arrived soon. One loan officer had already left, but the other said he already had the check cut and ready, just waiting for Peter to sign the papers.

If he ever showed up.

Mary Jane went over and sat beside Aunt May on the big, leather couch. She picked up a two-month-old *Newsweek* magazine with no intent of reading it. She just needed something in her hands.

Aunt May glanced up at her and smiled. "Did you find Peter?"

Mary Jane nodded. "He's on his way. He should be here any minute."

"Good," Aunt May said and nodded. "I knew he'd make it." Then she calmly went back to reading.

Mary Jane twisted her diamond wedding ring, a nervous habit that Peter had tried to get her to stop numbers of times. But for some reason she just couldn't shake the habit.

She looked around, trying to think of other things than waiting for Peter.

Too bad she couldn't sign the note. She would do it in an instant for Aunt May. But since she was out of a job they wouldn't take her credit. Peter had the job at the *Bugle,* and good credit, so he was the one to sign anything to do with finances at the moment.

As he said earlier, that might change by next month, but that wouldn't do Aunt May any good now.

But maybe there was something else she could do.

She twisted her ring and thought as the secretary continued to type and the minutes continued to click by.

David Ballard held Nancy close to him as they sat on the floor. His back was braced against the wall near the front door of the penthouse.

The big living room in front of him, once a fresh-smelling place where boring conversations were held over drinks, now smelled more like a slaughterhouse. Over two-thirds of the guests had died horribly since Carnage arrived.

Copper-smelling blood now filled the place with a thick, choking odor of death that not even the cool breeze from the open patio door could clear out. Blood drying in black spots and red streamers was splattered over everything as if an angry child had gone crazy with paints.

Over the last two hours the red and black monster had seemed to take great pleasure in killing randomly and without any sense at all.

Twenty minutes ago Carnage had selected one guy named Stephen, a writer of pretentious essays for small literary journals, to entertain him. Stephen was a short guy with a beard and a balding spot on the top of his head. Carnage had first made him recite a poem, then come and stand in front of him.

Carnage had asked Stephen questions for a few minutes about his life, his writing, and anything else that seemed to come to the monster's mind as Stephen stood before him.

Stephen, to his credit, except for the sweat pouring off his forehead, held his composure fairly well in the face of the wide mouth of razor teeth and the swirling and twisting tendrils of red and black whips that seemed to constantly be dripping off and whipping around Carnage's body.

Finally, in answer to a question, Stephen told Carnage his last published article had been ten thousand words about soup as a literary metaphor for life.

Carnage laughed. "Soup as life?"

Stephen, still sweating, nodded.

"The world will thank me for this," Carnage said.

A huge ax blade formed on Carnage's arm and, with a quick stroke, Stephen was dead.

Carnage picked up the body and walked toward the patio with it over his shoulder. "You want to see soup?" he said to the body. "I'll show you what is about to become the most dangerous soup of the century."

He draped the body over the railing of the penthouse, laughing. "Can you see it?" he asked the body, pointing at the food trucks below.

Then he laughed again.

David was getting real tired of hearing that laugh.

Carnage had been out on the patio ever since, watching the park and the crowds on the street below.

David glanced around at the bodies of his friends and at the few survivors doing exactly what he and Nancy were doing. Nothing.

Cowering.

Doing their best to not have Carnage notice them until help arrived or Carnage just got tired and left.

David could hear sirens from the street below. Maybe they would be lucky. Maybe help would come before they were all dead.

Nancy sobbed a little louder than normal and David quickly comforted her. She'd been in shock since their hostess had been killed right in front of her. From the looks of Nancy, she was going to need a lot of professional help if she survived this.

They all were.

"You!" Carnage said. "What did you say your name was?"

David looked up to discover that Carnage was pointing at him with a long tentacle that extended from the patio, across the living room, and hovered in David's face.

"David," he said.

The end of the tentacle turned into a finger and beckoned him to follow, like a woman inviting a lover into a bedroom.

David propped Nancy up against the wall and then on stiff legs stood, slowly following the tentacle as it retracted toward Carnage. He had to step over two bodies and walk through a puddle of blood before reaching the patio.

"You're a smart fellow," Carnage said as David stepped over a body in the patio doorway and then walked out into the cool fall air of the New York evening.

David said nothing. Without a doubt in his mind he knew he was going to die very quickly. He would give Carnage no pleasure in his death. It was the only pride he had left at the moment. It wasn't much, but he was going to hang onto it.

"You like to fly, David?" Carnage asked. Saliva

dripped out of the sides of his mouth and tentacles formed and retracted and then reformed all over his body.

David took a deep breath to let the cool air help clear his head. "I do my share of it on airlines, but I've never learned to pilot a plane."

"So you have no fear of flying?"

"No, I have no fear of flying," David said, his voice as steady as he could keep it.

"Good," Carnage said. "Because it's time for a distraction down below."

Tentacles whipped out and grabbed David and held him in a stranglehold before he even had time to react.

"Happy landings," Carnage said.

With a quick movement David found himself yanked off his feet and catapulted into midair as if a child threw a small doll. The last thing in his vision was Carnage's laughing face.

David tumbled, screaming as he fell, gaining speed, heading for instant death in the street below.

His mind was frozen.

He didn't want to die.

This was a stupid way to die.

"Brace yourself," a new voice shouted as sticky strands wrapped around him.

With a sharp snap his fall stopped and he swung inward toward the building. In the nick of time he got his hands in front of him to keep his head from smashing into the bricks. But the impact still knocked the wind out of him.

"Sorry about that," the voice said again as hands steadied him on the wide ledge between two windows. Then the hands grabbed him from behind and again, like he was a child's doll, picked him up and put him on the closest balcony.

David turned around expecting to see the ugly face of Carnage playing some trick on him, but instead looked into the blank mask of Spider-Man.

The breath David had been holding exploded from his mouth and his knees felt weak. He steadied himself on the railing of the open patio.

"Sorry to catch and run," Spidey said. "But I think I'm needed above."

David nodded uselessly as Spider-Man scrambled up the building and was gone from sight.

David's knees gave out and he collapsed onto the patio floor, gasping for air, the sticky webs tangled around his arms and stomach the only reminder that Spider-Man had been his savior.

Finally he managed to catch his breath enough to say two words to the cool fall air.

"Thank you."

CHAPTER 16

Dr. Catrall let the young policeman gently lead him down the hall away from the cell and into the more populated corridors of the Twentieth Precinct station. The noise of the station washed over him like a wave, but it didn't cut at his shell.

He felt like a zombie, with no energy.

Every time he even so much as blinked he could see the ugly face of Carnage, saliva dripping from his pointed teeth, laughing with that awful rotten breath.

And with every step he could feel Carnage touching him with those sharp claws, cutting him slowly, letting him watch his own blood through the pain until finally he told Carnage what he wanted to know.

The police who had found him had patched up the cuts and taken him first to the emergency room for the obvious wounds. It wasn't the cuts to his skin that hurt, but what Carnage had done to his mind and his ego that the doctors at the hospital couldn't fix.

Carnage had dug and cut at Dr. Catrall's soul.

And the doctor had sold out. He told Carnage what the vial's contents could do. What the vial's contents would do to other humans.

Carnage had clapped his hands together like a child with a new toy on Christmas morning. Then he had taken the briefcase with the vial of instant death and let Catrall live.

Let him live, turned him loose to torture himself with the knowledge of what was going to happen to thousands and thousands of people because of him.

Why hadn't Carnage killed him?

He was going to kill so many others. What difference would one more have made?

But Carnage had let him live and Catrall hated him even more for that.

"This way," the policeman said, pulling the doctor gently by the arm. Catrall's hands were handcuffed in front of him and the police had taken his belt and the contents of his pockets. As he walked he felt as if his pants would drop around his knees at any moment, so he held them up in front with his hands.

Catrall looked around at all the police and then at the young man in blue who was his escort as they entered the cage near the front door of the station. "Where are you taking me?"

"You're going to Bellevue Hospital's psychiatric ward for observation," the young cop said, almost apologizing.

Catrall nodded slowly, his mind accepting what

he had just heard. "Good," he said softly. "I think I need that."

The young cop gave him a sharp look and then sat him on a wooden bench just inside the holding cage. "We've got to wait here for transportation."

The kid checked the handcuffs to make sure they were still in place, than asked, "Anything you need?"

Catrall just shook his head no and stayed still, his hands folded neatly on his lap.

The cop stood near him, keeping an eye on him as the hustle and bustle of the station swirled around and past them. The noise and all the different conversations didn't get inside the shell Catrall had around him.

To his mind this station, life in general, had all become a giant, slow-motion nightmare.

Voices slurred, made no sense.

His vision blurred, colors mixing and swirling together.

Everything seemed to spin and then stop and then start spinning again.

Everything with the face of Carnage.

Red.

Black.

The pain.

He had never felt such pain, had no idea it was possible to endure. But he had. Somehow he had lived through it. Now he wished he hadn't.

The shouts from the front of the station broke slightly though the cloud as the guard standing over him moved a step away to get closer to what was going on near the front desk.

"Carnage has killed a room full of people," someone said.

Another said, "Where?"

"Central Park West and 82nd, right across from the *Bugle*'s Feed 'Em All wingding," someone else said.

The doctor surfaced from his own personal nightmare for a moment at the name of Carnage.

Shouting.

More voices.

Orders for more officers to deploy.

The name Carnage over and over and over again.

Dr. Catrall swam up out of the mists of his pain and self-pity to grab hold of one clear thought: *I need to kill Carnage! I need to get back my vial!*

The young cop had his back to him, his revolver sitting face-high in front of Dr. Catrall.

With a quick movement Catrall had the gun out with both handcuffed hands and pointed at the young man.

The kid spun around, holding up his hands, motioning for the doctor not to shoot.

"I need to get out of here!" Catrall shouted. "Now!"

"Gun!" two cops on the other side of the fence shouted. Everyone in the room went for their own guns while ducking behind counters and benches and walls.

Dr. Catrall swung the gun around, thinking he could hold the entire room at bay, force them to let him go so he could kill Carnage.

But it didn't work out that way.

The two cops closest to the sergeant's desk thought Catrall was going to fire. Each fired twice.

Four shots slammed into the Doctor's chest.

He spun around, the gun in his hand flying against the screen, as he went over backwards.

His blood splattered against the brick wall and over the bench in bright red stains. He tumbled to the floor, his head banging hard on the concrete.

The last thought Dr. Catrall had, as he lay on the cold floor and stared at the ceiling, was of Spider-Man upside down at his cell window.

He smiled at the thought.

"It's up to you, now," he said through a pink bubble of blood.

And as the young cop leaned over him with a horrified look on his face, Dr. Catrall closed his eyes and for the first time in years was at peace.

CHAPTER 17

Spider-Man had almost yanked his shoulder out of the socket when he caught the falling man out of the air three stories below the penthouse.

Somehow he had managed to catch the guy with two webs from above, snagging him around the waist and both legs, breaking his fall, while at the same time swinging him over against the building without turning him into bloody pulp on the bricks. His shoulder was going to hurt for days, but it was a small price to pay for the guy's life.

The guy still hit the building hard. But Spidey had jumped to his side to keep him from falling off the ledge. He'd then dropped the stunned man onto a nearby patio and scampered up the side of the building and onto the roof of the penthouse.

Looking over from the roof, he could see there was a body hanging over the patio rail, and another body of a woman sprawled half in, half out of the patio door. The man's body was the same one Peter had seen on the camera from the *Daily Bugle.*

But there was no sign of Carnage.

Silently, Spider-Man dropped down onto the patio when his spider-sense told him the way was clear. It hadn't taken him more than a few seconds to snag the falling guy and put him on the patio. Where had Carnage gone? He had to be close.

Real close.

But where?

Spidey poked his head around the edge of the door and studied the scene of slaughter inside the penthouse.

Blood was splattered everywhere, on almost every surface. Bodies lay scattered around the room like toys discarded by a child with too short of an attention span and way too much energy.

A few people were still alive, huddled against the walls and in corners, but not as many as were dead.

His spider-sense flared!

He ducked just as a huge spear flashed past and disappeared into the dark out over the park.

Spidey stepped directly into the opening of the patio door and faced Carnage who stood across the room, a wide-eyed woman held tight in his grasp.

The woman had big green eyes and brown hair, and seemed to be in total shock. Spidey couldn't imagine what demons were now roaming in that head.

"You keep throwing parts of yourself away like

that," Spider-Man said, "and there won't be anything left."

Carnage laughed. "Your fondest dream. Correct?"

Spidey nodded. "Ever since I first saw your ugly face."

Spidey slowly stepped farther into the living room, making a quick note of where the bodies lay and where the live ones were, too. He'd keep the fight away from them if he could.

"Well," Carnage said, "I hate to be such a stick-in-the-mud, but I have a dinner appointment."

"Yeah, right," Spidey said. "You do. Back in your cell. They're cooking your favorite tonight. Crow."

Carnage yanked hard on the woman whom he held around the neck and chest and her tongue stuck out slightly as she fought to breathe. "I don't think so. Now please stand aside or this pretty woman loses all future birthdays."

Carnage started toward Spidey and the patio door, his costume forming and melting weapon after weapon, none of which he fired.

Spidey backed up slightly, but didn't stay inside. Instead, he backed out onto the patio and to the right, moving close to the rail. He was about to make some joke about hiding behind a woman's skirts, then thought better of it. Carnage would kill the woman as easily as not. Provoking him to do so made no sense.

Carnage moved slowly toward the door, forcing the woman along in front of him. Her legs didn't seem to work and mostly he carried her.

Within a few seconds Spider-Man and Carnage faced each other on the patio with the woman still between them.

"So," Carnage said. "I saw that you enjoyed playing catch."

"Not really," Spidey said. "I would much—"

"Too bad," Carnage said. "I do love the game. Here. Catch!"

With very little effort or motion he flipped the woman high into the air and out over the railing into the dark night.

With instant reaction Spider-Man was on the rail. He hit the woman with two webs, one on the chest and one below the waist.

Then he yanked on both webs like a kid yanking on a kite string.

The arc of her trajectory suddenly changed before she could even gain the slightest momentum toward the ground. The web lines pulled her back toward the building.

Like being on a park swing, the two lines swung her under the patio of the penthouse and toward the balcony of the apartment directly below. Holding the web lines with one hand, he shot a mass of webbing with the other hand on the wall where she was about to hit.

She hit hard, but the impact was softened by the web pillow he'd hastily spun. For the moment, she was safe.

Spider-Man spun back to face Carnage just as the red and black costumed monster dove over the edge, heading down the side of the buidling toward the crowds below.

Spidey was over the patio rail right behind him.

Carnage must have assumed Spider-Man would spend more time saving the woman, because he knew Spidey was faster down a wall like this than he was.

As he followed, Spidey could see that Carnage had the vial tucked into a pouch on his back formed by his living costume. Spidey made a mental note to be careful not to hit him there and break the vial. That would be all he needed. A psycho pushed even more psycho with drugs.

In just a fraction of a second, Spidey was close enough. He stopped, planted his feet on the wall, and stood up straight as if the wall was just a normal floor.

With sure aim he hit Carnage with a web around the neck. Braced against the impact, Spider-Man yanked hard, pulling Carnage off the building and out into space over the street. He felt the tug on his strained shoulder, but ignored it.

Now was just not the time to worry about a few aches and pains.

"Your turn to play catch," Spidey said, letting go of the web so that Carnage flipped even farther from the building and out over the street.

Tendrils shot out from Carnage's costume, catching the railing of a nearby balcony and swinging him back in against the building, while at the same time he fired repeated darts off his costume at Spider-Man.

"Oh, I see you're good at that catch game, too." Spidey said as he easily ducked the darts. But the entire exchange gave Carnage another head start down the wall which Carnage instantly turned to his advantage.

On the street below, people and police shouted and scattered as Carnage hit the ground and ran for the park and the thousands gathered there under the lights.

Spider-Man hit the ground right behind him, took two of the biggest leaps he could and tackled Carnage with the standard tackle-from-behind, made so famous by old westerns on television.

The concrete felt very hard and rough as the pair of them tumbled. After one roll, Spidey was up and facing Carnage.

Carnage also rose up firing darts and axes and everything else he could think of from his costume.

It would have been fairly easy for Spidey to duck and avoid the shots, but if he did, some of them would hit the crowd.

So, instead of mearly ducking, he used webs, firing one after another to knock down each missile Carnage fired before it could hurt anyone.

Again Carnage got a head start, running away from Spider-Man, moving at full speed toward the food tables and the thousands gathered to feed the homeless.

"This is going to be a long night," Spidey muttered as he took off after him again.

CHAPTER 18

a pitched battle with Carnage, saving lives.

The least she could do to help was save Aunt May's house.

She hoped.

She went almost at a run out the front door of the bank and into the dark night on the streets of New York.

The Great Lawn area of Central Park was full of a very mixed group of people on the cool evening.

The large, open lawn smelled of freshly mown grass, and the rows of trees that surrounded the meadow were all the bright oranges and reds of fall. At least a thousand people were scattered in large groups around the meadow and in a larger crowd near the food tables. In the crowd, the homeless stood elbow to elbow with kitchen workers, reporters, and high society. It was a strange sight.

All were there for the same reason: to get something.

The homeless were there for the free food. All the free publicity promised them a meal different from what they normally scrounged on the streets or got in the shelters. So many of the homeless had worked their way to Central Park to see what all the fuss was about.

The kitchen workers filling the food preparation

trucks and staffing the preparation tables were there because they were getting paid. They didn't much care who they were feeding, or where, as long as the hours went on their time cards and the checks came regularly so they could make the rent and keep their own families fed.

The rich, the high society, the golden people of New York society, were there for the publicity and to help themselves feel good. Every so often a group of them would grab a homeless person, the shabbier the better, and pose, smiling, drinks in hand in front of the cameras. The pictures would later appear in the *Bugle* and other papers around the country and for the next month the rich would have a clear conscience while stepping over the homeless on the sidewalks. They *knew* they had done their good deed for the month.

They had written a check. They had shown up. What more could they do? Right?

But to a trained eye staring out over the party scene under the lights in the Great Lawn, there was one group of human beings obviously missing from all the great food and publicity. One group who hadn't bothered to show up: the people actually working on the problem of homelessness in America.

The social workers. The staff of the homeless shelters. The people who gave their time and energy every day for free, or almost nothing, to do their best to improve the lot of the needy of American society. They stayed away from Jonah's great event because they knew it was nothing more than a sham.

They knew it would do no good tomorrow or the next day or the next.

They stayed in the shelters working. They stayed on the streets helping find jobs.

They gave more than the rich could ever give. They gave their time. And their energy.

They didn't have any need for publicity. Most of the time they didn't want it.

They were the people who really cared that someone didn't have a place to sleep or enough to eat. They were the people who knew what to do with that caring and how to make a real difference.

They didn't come to the party. They weren't even invited.

But thousands of "golden" people *were* invited and they had shown up, each for their own reasons, each buying into the hype. So the meadow had been turned into a huge stage for them all to strut their stuff.

And now it had become a stage for Carnage to strut his killing ways.

Large, steel light towers had been set up on the four corners of the meadow and a taller one in the very center to flood the entire party with the same light that lit up a baseball field. "Plenty of light for the cameras," Jonah had said.

Plenty of light to see and be seen on a fall evening in New York City.

The food preparation trailers lined the pavement that ran along Belvedere Lake like a wall holding the homeless in the park. The area of the lawn closest to the trucks was lined with long rows of tables and benches.

The smell of the stew and fresh bread drifted over the thousands, making many of the rich wish they dared dig in next to the homeless. But the fear of getting *that* picture in the paper kept them at bay, kept them sipping their drinks, watching the homeless eat for a change, instead of the other way around.

A line of homeless people waiting for food had formed, stretching off into the dark trees to the right of the food trucks—the line went around the perimeter of the lawn in the same manner as the free Shakespeare-in-the-Park performance held every summer. Smiling, happy servers, mostly volunteers from the bridge clubs and country clubs, stood beside the food tables near the trucks and dished out huge helpings supplied by the professionals from the trucks and preparation areas.

Spider-Man, swinging at full speed across the street, watched as Carnage leaped onto a food truck and then over and into the crowd.

Spider-Man leaped to the top of the truck and stopped.

Carnage was cutting a swath through the crowd like a mower through tall grass as he headed for the dozen or so vats of stew lining the end of the food preparation tables. The vial was still in the pocket on his back, but it was now exposed, ready to be grabbed and dumped into the stew at any moment.

Spider-Man shook his head at the absurdity of it. It was almost funny. Why Carnage thought anyone would eat stew that he had poured anything into was beyond guessing. Maybe he planned on trying to sneak the liquid in. But Carnage sneaking *anything* in *anywhere* seemed opposite to his normal behavior.

But whatever the psycho-killer was thinking, ridiculous or not, he had to be stopped.

And quickly.

Spider-Man braced his feet and aimed his web-shooters carefully. If Carnage's focus was on the vial and the tubs of food, then the vial was what Spidey wanted.

He took a firm stance on the top of the truck and fired both web-shooters together. The right one hit Carnage exactly where Spidey had aimed it: the back of Carnage's knees.

The second shot hit the vial.

"Bullseye!" Spider-Man shouted.

As Carnage tumbled forward, his legs suddenly caught by the webs, Spidey yanked on the web stuck to the vial.

The deadly vial came loose, arching like a kite on the end of a string over the heads of the crowd and back at Spider-Man.

Carnage, tangled completely in the webs, went down rolling on the trampled grass and then regained his feet, his costume forming ten knives around his legs that cut the web to ribbons.

With a quick turn, Spidey hit the center light tower's steel frame about halfway up with a web and then jumped.

It would be close.

And his timing would have to be perfect.

Like a slow-motion shot of a bird, Spider-Man and the vial closed in on one another in midair.

Almost.

Almost.

He didn't dare drop it. Not in this crowd.

Finally, at the last moment, Spidey's outstretched hand grabbed the vial out of midair. Before he had even reached the tower he had it tucked safely inside his costume pocket. It made a very obvious and very large lump there. He couldn't fight Carnage carrying that. If it broke on his skin he'd become as bad as Carnage.

He forced that thought out of his mind.

Carnage screamed and started toward the tower at full speed, knocking people aside without paying the slightest attention to whether they were rich or homeless—not that he would have cared if he *did* pay attention.

"Tag, you're it," Spidey shouted as he scrambled up the tower to the flat part on the top. At least up here, if he kept Carnage busy, no bystanders would be hurt.

If they were smart enough to get out from underneath the tower, that is. Because Carnage was going to take a fall tonight if Spidey had anything to say about it.

As Carnage reached the base of the tower and started up, his costume swirling and twisting with anger, Spidey moved quickly to the center of the wooden platform where, for just a second, Carnage couldn't see what he was doing. Huge lights framed the four corners of the platform, leaving a twenty-foot open floor in the middle of plywood reinforced by steel.

He took the vial, wrapped it in a large wad of webbing to cushion it, and then shot it into the high branches of a nearby birch tree.

As it landed safely in the high branches and stuck, Spidey's spider-sense told him Carnage was about to join him on the platform.

With an instinctive move, Spidey jumped directly at where Carnage would appear over the edge of the platform.

He did a tight, tucked flip in midair, coming out of the spin with both feet planted firmly in the center of Carnage's chest, kicking as hard as he could.

Carnage was caught unaware just as he tried to climb onto the top of the light tower. The momentum of the double kick shot Carnage backwards and out into the air.

"Watch out below!" Spider-Man shouted.

But as he fell, Carnage spun and a rope-like tendril off his costume shot out.

Before Spider-Man could react to the warning his spider-sense gave him, the rope had grabbed him around the legs and yanked him right off the tower and into the air above Carnage.

The ground was a long way down and from this height the grass was going to feel like concrete.

Spidey's spider-sense was going nuts as Carnage wrapped him in more and more tendrils as they tumbled toward the ground. Spidey spun around, yanking off some of the tendrils. This fall was going to hurt real bad unless he did something, and did it quickly.

He spun again, ripping off even more of the tendrils of the red Carnage costume. With both arms suddenly free he shot two webs at the tower leg flashing by, and then held on as the momentum of the webs swung him and then Carnage toward the tower like two stones on the end of strings.

His strained shoulder screamed and he bit his lip against the pain.

Spidey was farther in the air but the length of the tendrils was enough to smash Carnage into the ground. Spider-Man swung between the tower legs and came up sitting on a support strut between the tower legs.

"Wow," he said, staring at where Carnage lay staring up at the night sky on the grass. "That must have hurt."

Carnage shook his head and quickly stood. He was only stunned.

"Always knew you had a hard head," Spidey said. "but I thought I had pounded some sense into it this morning."

The crowd that had backed away from the tower when the two started up now backed even farther away.

Carnage stood and shook his head. "Web-swinger, you're dead. I'm tired of you getting in the way of my plans."

Spidey laughed. "I thought you believed in chaos, Kasady. How can *you* make plans?"

Carnage just snorted as he started up the tower.

Spidey went up faster.

But not fast enough to outpace the tendrils.

Spidey's spider-sense went off just as a tendril wrapped around his leg and pulled. The warning gave him enough time to get a grip on a support girder near the top and the sharp pull from Carnage didn't dislodge him.

Instantly, Carnage was on him, pounding at him, his fists turning into steel hammers as they hit him over and over again.

One of Carnage's arms turned into a huge battle-ax and swung at Spider-Man's stomach.

Spidey managed to get his leg free just in time to dive behind another supporting beam.

The ax exploded as it hit the beam, like a grenade going off, sending Spidey tumbling over backwards.

Somehow he managed to snag one support with a web and swing around and back on the tower twenty feet below Carnage.

"I want that vial," Carnage said, climbing toward the top of the tower. "And since you're not carrying it, I assume it's up here."

The explosion had shaken Spidey, but his head was quickly clearing. As Carnage disappeared over the top and onto the platform, Spidey scanned the surrounding crowds. They were still far too close for comfort to the tower and the fight. But he didn't dare shout for them to get back and draw Carnage's attention to them.

From the top of the tower Carnage roared and

pulled one of the huge floodlights from its setting, sending electricity snapping and crackling around the tower. The light flew out into the air above the crowd.

"Oh, no," Spidey said.

People screamed and started to scramble out of the way. The light fixture had to be five feet across and as long as a car. It would crush a dozen people easily.

Instantly, Spidey hit the flying fixture with two web shots, then, wrapping both legs around the tower, he yanked as hard as he could, again ignoring the screaming pain in his shoulder.

Like a puppet, the fixture changed directions in midair, shooting back toward the tower. It missed smashing into the crowd by mere feet as it tumbled and exploded in a shower of glass at the base of the tower.

"Lucky that thing was lighter than it looked," Spidey said, stretching the muscles he had pulled in his back.

His spider-sense went wild.

He ducked and tumbled through the air toward the ground as a wave of pointed darts smashed into the girders he had been anchored to. He caught a beam and swung around and up onto a lower girder. He looked up.

Carnage was coming down after him.

And he looked very angry.

CHAPTER 19

The City Mortgage Company occupied a big stone building that looked to Mary Jane to be better suited to holding criminals. The gray stone blocks on the front dwarfed the double doors and made anyone entering feel small and insignificant. Mary Jane wondered if that had been a purposeful design feature, or more of an indication of the philosophy of the company.

Once through the double doors, she knew the answer with a quick glance around at the dark, imposing interior, huge desks, and old bank-like barred cages where customers could make payments. This was not a human place. This was a money place. Humans were just part of the problem.

Aunt May's tiny frail form seemed lost in one of the huge, overstuffed black chairs in the waiting area. She was sitting nervously with her hands in her lap, obviously wishing she could be in one of a hundred other places. When she saw Mary Jane crossing the dark tile floor her face lit up in a worried smile.

"I'm very concerned about Peter," she said as she struggled to pull herself out of the deep cushions. "It's just not like him to be late like this."

Mary Jane put a hand gently under her arm and helped her stand. "Oh, with his job," Mary Jane said, "this sometimes happens. He's under a lot of pressure, you know. Lots and lots of responsibility."

"I'm still worried," Aunt May said. Then she turned and looked up into Mary Jane's face, the obvious question not spoken, but clearly there.

"Where do we make your house payments?" Mary Jane asked.

"What?" Aunt May said, a look of confusion crossing her face.

"Do we need to go somewhere special to make the late payments and stop the repossession?" Mary Jane was smiling, but not too hard. First she wanted to get this taken care of before she let herself believe this might work.

Aunt May pointed at a man sitting behind a huge, dark wooden desk, across what seemed to be a half mile of carpeting. "That's Mr. Adams. He said all I needed to do was make the payment and then show him the receipt and he would stop everything." Aunt May smiled. "He was very understanding."

"So we make the payments at the window?"

Aunt May nodded. "But I don't see how—"

Her words were cut off as Mary Jane reached into her purse and pulled out a large wad of bills. "I think this will be more than enough to catch you up and even make next month's payment."

Aunt May stared first at the money and then up

at Mary Jane. "I don't know what to say."

Mary Jane really smiled for the first time in a while as she lightly hugged Aunt May. "You don't have to say anything. It was the least Peter and I could do for you."

Mary Jane slowly turned Aunt May and moved her toward the teller where she could make her late house payments.

And Aunt May did, her hands shaking as she counted out the money for each month, her eyes continuously darting to Mary Jane to make sure it was all right.

Mary Jane just kept smiling and smiling. Finally she understood how Peter felt after helping someone.

It felt good.

Real good.

The thousands of people who had come to Central Park for one form of entertainment this cool fall evening were now finding themselves with front row seats to one of the greatest battles of all time: Carnage vs. Spider-Man in New York City. Promoters could have sold tickets for large sums of money to this event.

The press was also having a field day. They had set up cameras to record a charity event, expecting the same dull and routine things that happened at high society gatherings. Suddenly the announcers and camera people discovered they were going live to the news departments around the world with news-breaking live coverage.

This was the most watched television event since the coverage of industrialist Tony Stark's kidnapping last month.

Spider-Man, on the other hand, would have much rather had the fight in a dark alley with no one watching. As far as he was concerned, all the bystanders were just more weapons for Carnage to use and more people Spider-Man had to somehow find a way to protect.

Carnage loved the coverage and the audience. His sworn duty was to spread chaos throughout the world and tonight, thanks to the televisions beaming into every house right at dinnertime, he was doing just that.

At the moment, protecting the bystanders was looking very difficult for Spider-Man. He found himself twenty feet off the ground, near the bottom of the steel light tower that sat in the middle of the open field. The tower was ringed by thousands of the rich and homeless of the city.

And Carnage was swarming down the tower from above, directly at him, taking aim like an angry swarm of red killer bees.

What to do?

Spidey quickly glanced around. If he went down and onto the grass, people would get hurt.

If he stayed put, Carnage would knock him off like so much dandruff on a black shirt.

So going up was the only choice. This fight had to stay on the platform above the crowd.

Somehow.

Spidey hit a steel crossbeam halfway up the tower with a web and jumped as hard as he could directly away from the tower and out over the crowd.

Below, a sea of faces tracked him like satellite dishes changing channels.

He twisted in midair to dodge two red spears shot by Carnage, then swinging, he let his momentum take him out and slightly up.

At the farthest point from the tower, where it would be logical to drop off onto the ground like a kid jumping out of a swing, he hit the underside of the tower's top platform with another web and climbed up that web as fast as he could, while his weight swung him back toward the steel beams.

"I want that vial!" Carnage shouted as he now scrambled back up the tower after Spider-Man.

"So you can go dump it in the food? How dumb is that?" Spidey shouted, then ducked as his spider-sense told him a long, razor-tipped tendril was about to cut through his head.

With a quick swing he was up and back on top of the tower's twenty-foot-square wooden platform. Enormous light fixtures, still aimed at the crowds below, occupied three corners of the platform, but two big cables that had run to the fourth light now lay twisted in the corner where Carnage had ripped out the fixture.

Suddenly, the platform started to shake.

"What the—"

Carnage exploded through the very center of the wood floor like a fish jumping out of the water. Wood and splinters shot out in every direction.

"Ever play king of the mountain?" Spidey asked as Carnage landed on his feet.

Without waiting for an answer, Spidey used both feet to smash Carnage solidly in the chest.

Carnage stumbled back and fell off the edge of the platform, catching himself twenty feet down with tendrils wrapping around the steel legs of the tower.

"I win!" Spidey said as he leaned over the edge and watched Carnage swarm back up at him.

"Your prize will be death," Carnage said, as nearly a hundred darts exploded off his body and directly at Spidey.

Spidey's instant reaction saved him, but not by much. He could feel the wind of the darts passing his back and legs as he dove for cover behind one of the huge light fixtures.

This time, as Carnage swarmed up over the side, firing as he went, Spidey swung underneath the platform and scampered upside down to where Carnage had climbed up. Every time he did this he felt like a fly on a ceiling, and this time was no exception.

In less than a second he was back on top of the platform behind Carnage.

Using both his fists like a sledgehammer, he smashed down as hard as he could on Carnage's shoulder, right at the base of the neck.

A blow like that would have sent a normal man into unconsciousness. Or more likely killed him.

The red and black monster went down to his knees, but was spinning around as Spider-Man went to hit him again.

Knives. Dozens of knives spun off of Carnage like water out of a sprinkler, slashing at Spidey from all sides, forcing him back and away, his every move barely avoiding the knives, barely avoiding being cut.

Closer and closer to the edge of the platform, Carnage's knife attack forced Spider-Man. He finally stepped out into space and dropped toward the ground, out of the line of fire from the sharp blades.

Below, the crowd was doing the same thing, scrambling to dodge the hail of blades from above. Some were not as lucky or as quick as Spider-Man and screams of pain filled the night air.

With a quick web to the bottom of the platform, Spider-Man stopped his fall and swung back up.

A direct attack sure wasn't going to do the trick. He needed something more.

Something that would stop this clown right in his tracks before anyone else got hurt or killed.

And Spidey knew just the trick.

Then his spider-sense screamed.

Hanging under the platform at the top of the tower, there was just nowhere to go.

Twenty different tendrils snaked around from the sides of the platform and grabbed Spidey as he swung and clawed to stay free of them.

The tendrils were just fast enough and gained just enough hold on him to pull him upward. Hard.

Right into the bottom of the wooden platform.

And then through it.

Spidey thought the world had come to an end. Sharp pain shot down his neck and through his right shoulder as his head and body were used as a battering ram to smash a new hole in the platform.

"Make a joke now!" Carnage said, laughing as he held Spider-Man up.

"Let's see. I used the breath one already!" Spidey said, and before Carnage could react, Spidey kicked up at the red chin.

Kick through! That's what he had always heard. Don't kick at something. Kick through it!

He did just that. Hard.

His foot caught Carnage squarely under the chin, sending him tumbling backwards onto the wood platform and stunning him just enough for the tendrils to drop Spidey.

Whirling as fast as he could, Spider-Man grabbed the two loose electrical cables from the ripped-out light.

Then, as Carnage tried to stand, Spidey shoved the exposed ends against the red and black, slithering costume.

The scream echoed out over the park and bounced off the surrounding buildings, to finally be swallowed by the dead leaves on the trees.

Sparks shot everywhere.

The smell was of burning rubber mixed with rotten fish.

"Wow!" Spidey said as he fought to hold the ends of the electrical cables against Carnage. "I thought your *breath* was bad."

Tendrils whipped around and around, slashing at Spidey's arms and the wires.

But Spidey held the high voltage against Carnage as the fireworks lit up the park and the red and black slimy costume writhed.

Finally, the symbiote around Cletus Kasady sputtered and popped like bacon grease in a hot iron skillet and disappeared in a small explosion of black, inky smoke that drifted up into the night sky and was gone.

With one final ear-piercing scream, Kasady slumped unconscious to the platform, no sign of the symbiote left.

Spidey tossed aside the two cables and quickly checked Kasady for signs of life. He was still alive, but not by much. The symbiote had taken the brunt of the high-powered charge, and retreated back into Kasady.

But knowing this symbiote, it would be back, given enough time. Kasady needed to be taken back to his cell quickly.

Spider-Man picked up Kasady and slung him over his good shoulder, wincing at the pain in his neck.

"Going down."

As Spidey slowly climbed down the tower with Kasady, he slowly became aware of a growing, rumbling sound building through the park.

His spider-sense wasn't tingling, so he wasn't in danger. He glanced around to see what was going on. And then he realized what it was.

Applause and cheers.

Thousands of people were giving him a standing ovation in front of the entire world on the six o'clock news. This kind of exposure sure couldn't hurt the old image.

Underneath his mask he smiled.

He dropped Kasady on the ground near an ambulance and was about to turn to the police standing nearby when he realized what he had thought of just a few moments before.

"Quick," he said to a nearby smiling man in a cardigan sweater. "What time is it?"

The guy glanced at his Rolex. "Six-twenty."

Spider-Man crouched next to Kasady and sat staring at the white, skinny body of the man who had almost killed him.

The man who had killed dozens of others earlier this afternoon.

The man who had cost his Aunt May her house. The very house he had grown up in.

Right then and there, sitting on that damp grass with thousands of people around, Spider-Man briefly thought of killing someone.

But the moment passed. Several police officers arrived, flanked by a cadre of Guardsmen, who approached with special restraints designed by scientists at the Vault.

"Take him away," Spidey said hoarsely. Then he shot a webline at one of the backstops on the softball fields that dotted the Great Lawn and swung up to the tree where he'd stashed the vial with Catrall's trigger. After snagging it and his camera, he leaped from the branch and shot another webline.

Spider-Man swung off eastward, the crowd's applause receding into the background.

CHAPTER 20

At a little after eight, Peter was shuffling slowly down the sidewalk just a block from Aunt May's home in suburban Forest Hills. The cool, clean air wasn't helping his mood as he kicked leaves out of his way. His shoulder and neck ached and he felt as if almost every muscle in his body had been strained. But the physical pain was nothing compared to what he was putting himself through mentally.

Ahead he could see the warm golden lights coming out of the front windows of the house he grew up in. Aunt May's house.

Mary Jane had left a note at their apartment telling him she and Aunt May were here and that he should join them. They were probably packing up all of Aunt May's things, all because he'd screwed up and not gotten to the bank in time. How could he have let his aunt down this much?

He just couldn't believe it had happened.

But it had.

For the tenth time he thought back over the afternoon, over the fight, over everything, looking for where he could have made the time. At one point he was even within two blocks of the bank while looking for Carnage. But he'd been so focused that he'd forgotten the woman who raised him.

Forgot she needed his help today more than any other day in her life.

And he had failed her.

Now he didn't even want to face her.

He would rather face five Carnages at once than go in that house at the moment. He supposed that was why he had taken the time to stop at the *Bugle* to drop off the pictures he'd taken. They were going to need the money even more now, having to help support Aunt May until those savings bonds matured.

And he had seen Jonah, in a desperate bid to overcome the bad publicity of the fight at his prize event, promise to fund a new, permanent homeless shelter in each of the city's boroughs. At least some good had come from Jonah's publicity stunt.

But Aunt May had lost her house.

He took a deep breath of the crisp air, kicked a few more leaves and then sighed.

"It's time to face the music," he said to the night.

He strode down the sidewalk, not allowing himself to look up at the house until he reached the front door. As he always did, he tapped twice and let himself in.

Mary Jane was in the living room and when she saw him she beamed and ran to him, jumping up and giving him a huge hug that hurt his neck.

Then she kissed him so hard he thought he was never going to get to come up for air.

Finally she broke off the kiss and before he could say anything, she held him at arm's length and looked him over. "Are you all right? From the scenes they replayed on the news it looked as if you got hurt. They were really hard to watch."

He rubbed his neck. "A little, but I'll be all right in a few days."

"I'm so proud of you," she said. "A lot of people could have been killed in that park today."

"I know," Peter said, but he couldn't look Mary Jane in the eye. "But I really let down Aunt May. How's she taking it?"

Mary Jane laughed. "She's in the kitchen baking cookies to celebrate."

"Celebrate?" Peter glanced around, realizing for the first time that he saw no packing boxes scattered among his aunt's furniture. "Why would she celebrate losing her house?"

Mary Jane laughed. "No, silly. She's keeping the house."

"But how?"

Mary Jane held up her hand and turned it back and forth until Peter finally noticed that her diamond wedding ring was gone. The one they had spent so much on.

She laughed at what must have been his obvious look of horror. "When I knew you were taking care of Carnage and weren't going to make it to the bank, I went to a pawn shop and hocked my ring. We were good shoppers when we bought it. The ring was worth enough to make all her back payments and next month's, too. But I didn't tell her what I did, so don't you dare either. She thinks we had the extra money in a few bonds I cashed in."

The relief Peter felt flooded over him. Aunt May's house was saved.

Mary Jane did it.

She saved it.

He hugged her so hard she yelped.

"But what about your ring?" Peter finally asked.

"We'll get it back when Aunt May pays us back from your uncle's bonds. The guy at the pawn shop gave me a redeeming ticket that's good until the end of the year."

Peter nodded, still not happy. But very, very relieved.

Mary Jane took him firmly by the shoulders, jarring his sore one, but he kept the pain hidden.

"Listen to me, Mister," she said, looking him directly in the eye. "It felt good helping Aunt May. You run around saving lives and the entire world almost every day. Today it was my turn to help out a little. To be your partner."

She smiled and kissed him. "Sometimes you just can't do everything, even if you are a super hero. Today I got to help out and, to be honest with you, it felt wonderful. Okay?"

Peter looked into the happy, twinkling eyes of his beautiful wife and smiled.

Then she laughed. And he laughed with her. And then she kissed him again and he kissed her right back, just as hard.

After a long time she took him by the arm and turned him toward the wonderful cookie smell coming from the kitchen. "I bet you haven't eaten all day, have you?"

"Not a bite," he said.

"Well, I'll fix you dinner. But you better be thinking real quick, Mr. Super Hero."

"Why's that?" Peter asked just as they reached the swinging kitchen door.

"Aunt May's going to wonder what happened this afternoon." She kissed him on the cheek. "I doubt the truth is going to cut it."

With that, she laughed and swung open the door to the most delicious smelling kitchen Peter could ever remember walking into.

Chocolate chip cookies. His favorite.

The next morning, as the rising sun started pouring in through the bedroom window, Peter clambered out of his warm bed. Mary Jane mumbled about his insanity when he got out and then swore at him for letting in so much cold air. He supposed he was crazy, but there was something he had to do before he could rest. He made a quick phone call, then donned his Spider-Man costume. He tucked the professor's vial tight in his pouch and then, favoring his sore shoulder, swung out the window heading downtown.

He had one more task to complete.

The vial, a time bomb ticking away at the sanity of humanity, rode against his stomach. He at least owed Doctor Catrall the favor of finding it a safe home.

Ten minutes later, Spidey approached the gleaming skyscraper of Four Freedom's Plaza. Like all of New York's most famous skyscrapers, Freedom's Plaza had a distinct look, in this case the stylized "4" etched into each corner of the building's upper floor walls.

Those numbers, as well as the building's address, were symbols of the building's owners and most famous occupants: the Fantastic Four.

A single figure stood in the center of the building's roof, a trench coat covering his dark blue uniform, with white trim and a "4" similar to the ones on the building emblazoned on the chest: Reed Richards, a.k.a Mr. Fantastic, the FF's leader and one of the most renowned scientists the world had ever known.

As Spidey landed on the roof, he remembered the first time he came to this site, back when it was the Baxter Building. He'd only been Spider-Man a short while, and tried to join the FF in the hopes of making extra cash. That didn't pan out, but he had worked with the quartet dozens of times over the years and they had proven to be among the finest allies he'd ever had in the super hero game.

He walked toward Reed, one hand holding the vial in his pack like a mother would cradle a new child. He could feel the tension in his sore shoulders and arms. It would feel very good to have this finished.

Reed stuck out his hand, and Spider-Man shook it with his free hand. "Nice job last night," he said with a warm smile.

"Thanks. I think I got lucky."

Reed's face turned more serious. "Are you all right? From the tape I saw, it looked like you took a beating."

Spidey moved his shoulder up and down a little, feeling the pain. "Actually I ache in more places than I knew were possible to ache, but I'll recover."

"Good. I wish we would have been able to get back to help you out. But I'm glad you didn't need it."

"It would have been nice to have your help, but what's important is that this is safe." Spidey withdrew the vial and gently handed it to Reed.

Reed took it and held it up in the faint morning light. "So this is what the fuss was all about."

Spidey laughed. "Besides Carnage getting loose, I suppose so. Yeah, supposedly just touching that stuff can drive a human totally over the edge and into a killing machine. Tell you what, let's not test it."

"Carnage was going to place this in the food?"

"Yeah," Spidey said. "I guess he thought people would still eat the stuff after they saw him do it. The guy never really has functioned on all four cylinders."

"Lucky for us," Reed said. He pulled a container out of the trench coat's pocket. He pressed a button, and it opened with a hiss. Reed carefully placed the vial inside and closed the case.

As he did so Spidey could feel himself relaxing.

"I'll make sure this gets into the vault downstairs," Reed said.

"I'd feel happier if you could find a way to destroy it."

Reed nodded. "So would I. We'll see what we come up with."

"Thanks for taking it," Spidey said. He really meant that more than he could say.

"We'll keep it safe."

Spider-Man nodded. With a wave of thanks to Reed, he stepped toward the edge of the roof. He paused, inhaling the cool morning air through his mask and reveling in the promise of a beautiful fall day.

"Would you like a ride somewhere, son?" Reed called after him, apparently mistaking his hesitation for indecision.

Spidey turned and smiled. "No thanks. I know a short-cut home right over the top of that building." He pointed at a nearby high-rise. "I'm going back to bed."

Reed laughed. "I'd say you deserve it."

Spidey nodded to himself as he hit the building with a web. He did deserve it. And if he had his way, he was going to sleep through most of the day and Mary Jane was going to join him.

And he had his way.

David Michelinie's path was chosen at an early age. While other children of the 50s dreamed of becoming cowboys, movie stars, and astronauts, David confidently announced that *he* was going to be a writer. (As if wearing eyeglasses from age eight wasn't enough to attract every bully in his native Nashville, Tennessee.) Nevertheless, though battered and bruised, he reached maturity with enough enthusiasm intact to make his dream come true, publishing one previous novel (*The Man Who Stole Tomorrow*) and having a short story included in the recent anthology *The Ultimate Spider-Man*. He's also written over 500 comic book stories, telling tales of such stalwarts as Spider-Man, Iron Man, Swamp Thing, the Avengers, and, currently, Superman. An appreciator of classic Writer Clichés, he lives with cats (Merlin and Pandora) and, to the thinly-veiled concern of friends and family, is still not quite sure what he wants to be when he grows up.

Dean Wesley Smith has been a Spider-Man fan since issue #1, so much so that in the mid-70s he started his own comic store, finally selling it to go into writing full time. He is also the editor and co-publisher of *Pulphouse: A Fiction Magazine* and has four Hugo Award nominations for Best Editor. In 1989 he won a World Fantasy Award with his wife, Kristine Kathryn Rusch, for their work on *Pulphouse.* He has written or cowritten a half-dozen novels and over sixty short stories, including a *Star Trek: Deep Space Nine* novel, an *Aliens* novel, a *Star Trek: The Next Generation* novel, and a Spider-Man short story. But even with all that, he still reads Spider-Man comics every month.

Rocketed to Earth as an infant, **James W. Fry** escaped the destruction of his home planet and grew to adulthood in Brooklyn, New York. In 1984, seduced by the irresistible combination of insane deadlines and crippling poverty, he embarked on a career as a freelance illustrator. James's credits include *Star Trek* and *The Blasters* for DC Comics, *Moon Knight* and *Slapstick* for Marvel, *SilverStar* for Topps, and book illustrations for several *Star Trek: The Next Generation* young adult novels and *The Ultimate Spider-Man.* Himself a leading cause of stress-related illness in editors, James's greatest unfulfilled ambition is to get one full night of guilt-free sleep.

Keith Aiken is a talented young inker, whose past credits include work on *The Silver Surfer* for Marvel and the novel *Spider-Man: The Venom Factor* for Byron Preiss Multimedia Company. He lives in Sacramento.